THE AUTHOR

Susanna Mitchell was born and educated in
Ireland. She has worked with a television
company in Belfast, in advertising in London,
and now lives in Hampshire with her husband
and two daughters. She has published a
number of short stories and poems, together
with two novels, *The Token*, 1984, which was
shortlisted for the *Yorkshire Post* Book of the
Year prize, and *The Christening*, 1986.

Also by Susanna Mitchell

The Token
The Christening

THE COLOUR
OF
HIS HAIR

Susanna Mitchell

ALLISON & BUSBY

First published in Great Britain in 1994 by
Allison & Busby
an imprint of Wilson & Day Ltd
5 The Lodge
Richmond Way
London W12 8LW

ISBN 0 74900 255 7

Typeset by TW Typesetting, Plymouth, Devon.
Printed and bound in Great Britain by
Mackays of Chatham PLC, Chatham, Kent

To
Paul and Margaret Buxton

Oh who is that young sinner with the handcuffs on his wrists?
And what has he been after that they groan and shake their fists?
And wherefore is he wearing such a conscience-stricken air?
Oh they're taking him to prison for the colour of his hair.

'Tis a shame to human nature, such a head of hair as his;
In the good old time 'twas hanging for the colour that it is;
Though hanging isn't bad enough and flaying would be fair
For the nameless and abominable colour of his hair.

A. E. HOUSMAN

This year my father agreed at last to sit for a formal portrait, but refuses to hang it with the rest until he hands over to Jim and retires from the business completely. My father knows nothing of painting, and I think he is quite satisfied, and even proud of the thing, which has no artistic merit and bears small likeness to the sitter. In this it follows tradition, no talent is to be found adorning the walls of the boardroom, but it saddens me to see the crude and lifeless image that is to be his memorial. McMurtry men are not comely. Generations have not changed the spade-shaped face, nor the close set eyes with the fleshy nose beneath them, and these the painter has captured, but a basic gentleness shines through my father's features, giving them an endearing quality that is quite absent in the portrait. It is also absent in Jim, whose looks otherwise mirror my father's and bring him much satisfaction, for he knows that local opinion holds them both to be fine big men, and that this is a flattering accolade beside which refinement of feature is of no importance whatever. If a man is large and strong he is judged a handsome fellow though he be as plain as a ploughshare, and his bulk speaks well for his status. In our native Killycreel, it is certainly noticeable that the people who stay in the Old Town are on average very much smaller than those resettled down the hill in the relative prosperity of what is described as the New Town.

1

The Old Town is considered an obsolete place, a slum, an affront to the district. Indeed it has been scheduled for demolition for years, and though funding has not been forthcoming, successive local councils and public opinion for once unite in saying it ought to go. With the special contempt Ulster people reserve for the simple and the time-worn, they dismiss the traditional terraces of local slate and stone, and the steep streets that run between them, some still unevenly cobbled, that lead to the rank village green on the side of the hill, where the rubbish piles up by the broken pump and the horse trough. 'You wouldn't put tinkers into it', they say, 'a dirty old place like that, what's worth the saving?' – no shopping precinct, no fine new bungalow, no modern housing or spacious concrete car park, not a plate glass porch, nor even a picture window! A disgrace altogether, until you get to the Convent.

The Convent is like a frontier post. It lies on the edge of the Old Town but blandly and grandly detached from it, with its smart new extension and steel window frames, and the neat cement rendering that has obliterated all traces of weathered granite and carved architrave. Such style simply serves to underline the grievance of those who must pass it each time they climb the hill, grumbling and rancorous, their backs turned on supermarket, on neon-lit café, on amusement arcade, on the new dual carriageway that stops short of the river, and the half-built paradise of the council estate that straggles out over the valley. As seen from the Old Town, the New Town embodies a dream of prosperity that is out of its grasp, and when seen from the hill, the distinction shows up very plainly. As I joined the queue at the roadblock on the outskirts of the town, the mean winter light was fading, and the street lamps divided the valley as though serving two separate settlements. I could see the sprawled outline of the New Town lying beneath me picked out in green fluorescence, while on the far side of the river's mouth, the mound of the

2

Old Town, by contrast, seemed lit by candles, glimmering yellow across the water. The horizon was swallowed in rising ground.

As I sat there looking down, the familiarity of the view made the journey that lay behind me appear curiously insubstantial. The long and tedious drive to Liverpool from London, the uncomfortable night on the ferry, the business meeting in Dublin began to fade from my mind, obliterated by this place where they had no significance. For a moment my whole identity, the life that I had made and the tenets by which I lived it, began to grow vague and uncertain, smothered under the weight of my childhood.

With an effort I turned my eyes away from the valley, and looked instead at the patient row of drivers to whom a roadblock was commonplace: here, it simply replaced the delay you used to endure at the customs post a mile or two back at the border, a building blown up so regularly by the local IRA that it has at last been abandoned. It had long been redundant anyway; no one smuggles domestic contraband from the South to the North these days. The traffic is all the other way and is greatly to Killycreel's benefit; such trade is the one advantage of being a border town. Everything is cheaper than in the South, clothes, shoes, food, drink, toys, hardware. Day trippers, eager for bargains, pour in by the coachload and are viewed with condescension by the prudent shop proprietors who think them a down-at-heel rabble and watch them narrowly as they grab and jostle in pub and store, filling plastic bags and holdalls and shopping-trolleys and baskets and carrycots and prams – like a crowd of drunken tinkers, in the tradesmen's expressed opinion, but God love you, you can't expect better coming from the other side! Yet despite this depressing verdict, nobody refuses their custom. You learn to respect good money if you live in Killycreel, though you may despise those who spend it.

As I waited now, one of these buses, heading homeward across the border, passed me in the southbound lane. It vibrated with sounds of revelry, red faces and upturned beer-cans could be seen at every window; shouting, laughter, snatches of song drifted over the heads of the sober queue and the soldiers who crouched in the ditches with machine-guns trained on the roadway. I knew before I could see the badges on their berets that this was no English roadblock. English soldiers are strained and anxious and lack the ability to chat with the local inhabitants, since they have no means of distinguishing the upright from the murderous. The territorial eye, on the other hand, has been trained from birth to recognise the difference between one ruffian and another, and this well-developed trait makes the atmosphere more convivial and ensures that the traffic flows faster. Where's the sense in delaying your own ones when you know you can spot the Taigs?

As I watched the car in front of me, I wished I did not know these things. As a stranger I might feel stress at finding myself in a roadblock at all, but at least I would be encouraged by the jovial, good-natured attitude of the soldier just ahead who was sharing a joke with the driver. As I lowered my window I heard him slap the roof of the car in farewell, with a hearty 'Be seeing you, Billy!'. He was still smiling as he approached me, taking in my English number plates and my respectable air of solid middle-class affluence, and correctly assessing me harmless. He looked at my driving-licence in a perfunctory way, and observed my unaccented voice with an alteration of manner that classified me immediately as a hoity-toity fool who could not be expected to realise that decent Ulster people did not use the Dublin ferry when they could cross by Belfast.

'And where are you headed for, Madam?' The 'Madam' was derisory, a friendly derision for visitors who spoke so la-di-da that you scarcely could keep from mimicking them. Irrationally, it stung me. The mockery seemed to underline my estrangement from Killycreel, and reminded me unpleasantly of the sense of alienation that always crept in to destroy the warmth I would have liked to feel.

'I'm going home,' I said shortly, 'to Dunvarden.' And added deliberately as if *he* were the stranger, 'It's just outside Killycreel, on the other side of the bridges.'

I looked up at him balefully, and the childish hurt must have shown in my voice, for he glanced back at my licence, which was of English issue and in my married name, and then peered in at the window, his whole demeanour different.

'If it's not the wee McMurtry girl!' He shook his head in shame. 'And I never recognised ye! And you the spit of your Mammy!' He laughed, and then added solemnly, 'Well, but you're welcome home. It's glad I am to see you.' His warmth was entirely genuine. He would have extended his hand to shake mine in formal courtesy had he not already been holding both his Sterling and my licence. My Englishness was forgiven. I reflected uneasily that this cordial response to the family name from the agents of law and order had become a lot more conspicuous ever since my brother Jim had stood in the council elections as a Democratic Unionist. Whatever my father's opinions had been, they had not affected his son, and Jimmy was running McMurtry's now to all intents and purposes. Besides I was soon to discover that the incidents of last week were regarded as lesson enough to be learned by an old man in his sixties. That was what you got for being too soft, no point in rubbing it in.

'I was sorry to hear of your trouble.' As he spoke, his name came back to me. Owen Nesbit, Preacher Nesbit's son. His father, an amiable man when he served in his draper's shop during the week, used to don his blue suit of a Sunday and station himself on the seafront every weekend, year after

5

year, yelling hellfire at the populace. Everybody knew Preacher Nesbit, and although no one actually listened to him, he was always greatly prized as a colourful local character and a feature of Killycreel's Sabbath. Half the town had walked at his funeral when he eventually died. But the days were over and done with when such jokes might be shared between neighbours. An eccentric could no longer raise a smile across the divide between opposing religions and conflicting national interests. The Preacher's sons had inherited his convictions, but could not find satisfaction in simply declaring them to deaf ears and jocular comment. Zealot and audience alike had found new roles to play, and Owen's Sterling rifle had replaced his father's Bible. Those not with you were against you.

'You'll be glad to be back, I don't doubt,' he handed me my licence, 'and a good day you've got for the journey.'

I nodded. The damp filled my body with familiar lethargy, and my eyes ached from straining through the fog and the blear of the rain-streaked windscreen. The mist that had swaddled the morning was gradually turning to rain, a thin quiet drizzle that coated Owen's uniform with a rime of delicate irridescent grey; but the air was mild, and I knew that the television had revealed that England was blanketed with snow. 'Powerful warm for the time of year,' persisted Owen, and I gave the mandatory answer, 'A fine soft day!' so that we might part united in an unspoken agreement that the climate in Northern Ireland put everywhere else to shame.

I had switched off my headlamps in order to conform to the rules of the roadblock and now in the dying December day, pale objects gleamed eerily as though covered with a luminous paint: men's faces showed stark and waxen above bodies that merged with the hedgerows; the sides of the darkening road were delineated by litter, soiled wrappings and empty beer-cans caught the last of the light and glowed whitely, like a regiment of curb stones. Ahead, the army vehicles loomed featureless as boulders, slewed out at staggered intervals so that they turned the road into a miniature slalom course. I zigzagged bleakly through them, lifting my hand in the token salute that I knew was expected from me as a traveller who had been greeted with such gusto by a comrade. 'You'll be glad to be back.' I turned up my lights and drove down to Killycreel with a spasm of claustrophobia that shamed me by its disloyalty.

I tried to think of my father, though the picture conveyed little comfort. If he had been out of hospital I would have turned east to the quay where our solid Georgian business house still stands beside the harbour. He would have been pleased to see me. There would have been cups of tea in his shabby vault of an office that is known in the firm as the Boardroom, and whose ugly and functional fittings have remained exactly the same since the days of my great-grandfather; they are, after all, still serviceable. The McMurtrys have always been frugal, obstinately resistant to change. The linoleum is worn to its backing, the tall windows are uncurtained, their glazing bars and shutters still painted the liverish brown beloved of Victorian businessmen. As a gesture towards progress the elegant marble fireplace has been roughly boarded in and a double-barred electric fire fixed permanently in its centre. The wallpaper is original, and above my father's desk hang several prints of Killycreel as it was in the 1830s, with its famous network of canals spread below the Old Town on the hill, and the docks and wharfs thronged with shipping round the busy estuary where our new premises dominated the rest of Merchants' Quay.

The canals had been the basis of Killycreel's prosperity. Inland to north and westward they had carried the timber and coal, the bales of cotton and woollen yarn; the tea, sugar, spirits, tobacco; the foodstuffs; the slate and tallow, the un-

7

wrought iron and lead that provisioned half the Province. Local produce was brought to the harbour, both for dispersal inland and for the export trade: linen cloth and livestock, butter and pork and bacon, potatoes and milled oatmeal, flax and barley and wheat all flowed out to England and Scotland, to Holland and North America. On the East Coast only Belfast had stood to rival Killycreel. This rivalry was to prove fatal. Belfast expanded voraciously. Killycreel was little affected by the rise of its linen trade, but the siting of the huge shipyards there at once eclipsed its position, and as Belfast Lough grew in consequence, so Killycreel's eminence waned. But though poorer, it did not grow smaller: instead, its population increased as its trading potential and its commerce fell away. The industrial revolution had disrupted the rural economy, and men settled in desperation round the port at Killycreel where employment had once been so plentiful. But the widespread growth of the railways was to cause irreversible damage to the standing of the town. Waterways were abruptly outdated. The canals that had been essential to the distribution of produce and the import and export trade were suddenly rendered obsolete. Firms moved north or went out of business. Merchant ships forsook the harbour and used the port at Belfast where their cargoes could be delivered with less expense and trouble. By the time my father took over the firm, McMurtry's alone remained, with its coal boats and its timber yards and the private railway-siding it had built to shunt the merchandise to the waiting railway trains.

Now even this innovation in turn has been discarded. The branch lines have closed, goods travel great distances by road. My father, with grim tenacity, has bought a fleet of lorries. For five generations McMurtry's has traded from Killycreel and deserves its reputation for hard-headed business acumen. It has not been afraid to move with the times, though its very survival lies in the thrift and lack of pretension that makes it seem so conservative. James McMurtry & Son. Shipping Merchants. Importers of Timber & Coal. Established 1820. The original letter headings and signs carry with them a vintage air that makes you think of hansom cabs, frock coats and penny farthings. Although there is no portrait of that first enterprising James who brought little more than his shrewd wits from Scotland and prospered so fruitfully on Ulster clay, you can see his son there on the boardroom walls, complacent in faded sepia; and his grandson in oils, wearing round his neck the insignia of Mayor; and his great-grandson, my grandfather, heavy-jowled in his high white collar, with the sash of the Orange Order stretched proudly across his breast.

I turned inland and edged the car slowly along the crowded main street. Christmas was coming and it was market day. The sale yard was full, and despite the no-parking restrictions, mud-splattered trailers blocked side roads and alleyways, spilling straw and dung on to the pavements. The pungent odour of manure and terrified animal seeped its way into the press of shoppers and hung there sourly. Above me, huge plastic discs, wired over the road, alternately represented singing angels and cherry-cheeked Father Christmases; each one was surrounded by a ragged cordon of light-bulbs, too high to be stolen, as those on the Christmas tree appeared to have been, but also too high for replacement, so that spent filaments, like missing teeth, broke the symmetry of the circles that winked on forlornly, eclipsed by the glare of the shopfronts underneath.

The shops overflowed. Security men are hard pressed around Christmas, and although they reduce their precautions to a cursory glance into bags and a pass with their metal detectors, the queues still form on the pavements: bedraggled girls, barely full-grown themselves, already with

9

toddlers and prams; dour women with swollen ankles and scarves tied over their curlers; gaggles of unemployed youngsters and prosperous farmers' wives all coughed and nudged and shuffled in the persistent mizzle. Here and there I caught sight of a face that I knew, disturbingly familiar and yet so subtly distorted by intervening time, that I had to glance back to make sure who it was. I always find this depressing. I wondered if Owen had felt sad too when he greeted me just now – a girl he had known in his schooldays two decades ago, peering out at him from a face that, until the last moment, he had failed to recognise.

I drove on through the square where the school children swarmed round the waiting country buses. The gym-slips we wore in my day were gone, but the colours were the same: the grey and red of St Malachy's High, royal blue for St Christopher's Secondary, and then, boarding different buses, the sober bottle-green of St Christopher's opposite number, the Protestant Intermediary, and the unbecoming maroon and gold of Killycreel Grammar School.

It need hardly be said that there is no law that segregates public transport. The children have taken the matter in hand without apparent strain. It is simply another fact of life: if you're Catholic you form Catholic transport, and likewise Protestant pupils make up a Protestant bus, as a matter of course. What else would you do? There is no room for conjecture. It clearly stands to reason that you travel with your own kind – as you pray with them, live with them, learn with them; love and marry and breed with them, and if called upon, fight, kill and die for them. Your own sort. Your own faith. Your own tribe.

Those not with you are against you. I could not see the faces of the gold-and-maroon-clad children who filled the bus ahead, but then they did not need faces; for me, they already had them. Kenneth Corkey and Marion Muldrew. Betty

10

Cooper, who shared my desk but refused to come to my wedding. Ruth McAuley and Shirley Annett. Brian Burns, who was known to cheat in exams but is now held in great acclaim as a Free Presbyterian minister. Johnny Chambers. Mervyn McKee and little Deirdre Adams who eventually married each other, and whose only son followed his father into the RUC and was killed last year by a car bomb before he reached his twenties. Big Dick Bond and bigger Joe Baker, teamed bully-boys even then, and now heavily into protection, so I understand from my brother, who alludes to them from time to time as the sort of friends you need. And of course there was Heather Ryan; but Heather-the-child has faded, overlaid by the matronly Heather that I now find married to Jim, and who makes me feel either defensive or insultingly patronising.

The bus stopped in front of the Orange Hall, and I passed it thankfully. Though I knew the relief was irrational I felt better with it behind me. The children affected me not so much with nostalgia for the past as regret for lost allegiance, for the solid beliefs I might still have embraced had I been allowed to stay at home and take that bus each day till my education was over. It would have been so simple. But Jimmy and I were not left to complete our schooling in Killycreel. Jim moved on to attend Campbell College, as his father had done before him. Father always declares that Campbell runs like an English public school, but since there were no English schoolboys, this had little impact on Jimmy, who settled in immediately, emerging with his views on his homeland and the world at large not noticeably different from those of his contemporaries at Killycreel Grammar School.

My mother, however, grew bolder in the five years that lay between Jim and myself. She wished for my social advancement and, when I reached my teens, she sent me to school in England. It was too late to change her own standing, but if

11

I were to gain a foothold in the small, closed community of upper-class Anglo-Irish at the top of the social ladder, she saw that I must be anglicised. The effect of Campbell on Jim, and indeed upon my father, showed that this was unlikely to happen unless I left the country. I am sure she did not foresee that this might change more than my accent and my consequent eligibility. To this day, I do not think that she knows why I rapidly ceased to be a daughter she could be proud of and became a hostile stranger whose visits held little for her but confusion and dismay, growing deeper at every meeting. Outrage and disappointment. Betrayal and public shame. In a way it would have been easier if I had stopped reappearing, at least I would not have embarrassed her. You can better explain away a daughter who simply has vanished than excuse one who keeps returning, first married to a Catholic, now openly living in sin, in the face of everyone's notions of decency and propriety, and shocking both friends and relatives with her preposterous views on politics and religion and the local situation. Yes, it would have been less awkward if I had stayed away.

Yet on the other level, the level on which we now seldom meet, so seldom that sometimes I wonder if it still exists at all – there, surely, my absence would have been worse than my aggravating presence? Perhaps not. In any case, I was late. I should have telephoned. I took the old road off the new roundabout that now stands at the end of the main street, and left the school bus far behind me on the steep gradient of the hill.

The road that leads north up the rising ground between Killycreel and Dunvarden is wider than it used to be, and the few undistinguished trees that grew along its verges have been cut down in the widening. In their place, a rash of bungalows has erupted on either side, each one starkly surrounded by a driveway of bare black tarmac. They are much in demand, these bungalows with their huge windowpanes, and their chimney-breasts faced with coloured stone and their glaring plastic roof tiles. Each year there are more and more of them. Already, seen from the air, the whole countryside seems to have sprouted them as a summer lawn sprouts daisies. The old farmhouses and cottages are pulled down or fall into decay.

My brother has recently started to build in the high fields below Dunvarden. Ever since his marriage to Heather he has lived in Killycreel in the last residential town-house to survive from the early heydays of trading. An unheeded reminder of Georgian grace, it was the McMurtry's first home when the family settled in Killycreel, and until now has served to good purpose. When great-grandfather built Dunvarden for its beautiful view of the sea and its air of country prosperity, the town-house was reallocated as the rightful preserve of the eldest son. With its frontage on the Mall, which runs parallel to the old towpath behind the back yards of the High Street shops, and its garden stretching behind it towards the empty moorland, it must once have been very lovely. Even twenty years ago, it remained a convenient and elegant house in harmony with its surroundings, a fine home for a young married couple. But now the New Town has spread, has engulfed it in gimcrack buildings. The one-way traffic flow has transformed the Mall into a main thoroughfare. The marsh meadow behind has been vested to make room for the new telephone exchange. The terrace to its left has been gutted to first floor level and turned into a shopping centre. To its right is a furniture warehouse. The Ulster bus depot occupies the side road by the small strip of land that is all that remains of the orchard. No one can blame Jimmy for moving. I have watched his new bungalow grow, from the first raw gash on the hillside to its present ill-favoured proportions, without

13

mentioning how it offends me. This is Jim's country now, not mine. I have no right to show indignation or grief when I see its neglect and disfigurement.

It is easy to miss our steep turning these days. O'Hagan's is still on the corner, but somehow it is diminished. Not so very long ago it used to be a landmark, the only building worth mentioning. 'Turn left when you come to O'Hagan's pub, you couldn't miss that if you tried – a fine big place, with a petrol pump and the bus stop right fornent it . . .' But now it is nothing remarkable, scaled down by the width of the road and eclipsed by the new filling station. The bus stop too has been altered, and sports its own concrete shelter some fifty yards to the right, so that travellers have no need to retreat to O'Hagan's porch for protection. Only when I look down upon it from our high side road can I see it restored again to the prominence of place that it held in my child-hood, as the first stagepost of my journey to the school at Killycreel.

I used to bicycle every day to the bus stop at O'Hagan's, between the loosely piled grey stone walls and the hedges of hawthorn and whin. Whin: I call it gorse now, but whin it was then, great mounds of it springing up in the fields and ditches with hardly a prickle of green showing through the extravagant bulk of flowers, the harsh flamboyant yellow. On wet summer days I could stand by the road in my bright oilskin cape, so camouflaged by the bushes that Colm would pass straight by me. Blazing whin, and unlucky hawthorn that you must never bring home lest the Devil enter with it and stay in the house for a twelvemonth. I found it very disquieting that the Devil should choose for his own such a blithe and innocent-seeming flower, though Nanny Magennis told me that he wore many fair disguises when he wanted to enter a home.

I learned much about deception from studying Colm's

14

grandmother. When we were alone together, she was fierce and acid of tongue, with a high hard voice that shrilled out commands and nagged and complained without ceasing, but, by the time I was seven or eight, I began to be aware of the cringing obsequious manner that she used when she spoke to my parents. I heard with amazement the honeyed tone, saw the sweet deferential smile with which she greeted my mother. It was sinister, but fascinating. At first it seemed Nanny Magennis could be nothing but a witch, a witch of the Hansel and Gretel kind, one moment the grateful tenant of your parents' half-derelict cottage, the next a vindictive crone who in some unidentifiable way was deeply disposed against you. But soon I left fairy-tales behind, and it became plain to see that she was simply devious, deliberately two-faced and cunning, and that my poor parents believed in the face that she chose to let them see.

I knew she respected no one. Waves of spite vibrated around her when she cursed and gossiped with neighbours, or whispered mysteriously with the curious friends that Uncle Matt brought now and then to the cottage, and I sensed this all the more strongly when she fawned on my family. Yet the ill will was not directed at me and I knew myself exempt from it: what I did not know then, was that nothing but her peasant's love of the child shielded me from her resentment of everything I stood for – my religion, my family's politics, the alien blood in my veins, my privileged social position. Her hatred of me was dormant, briefly suspended and held in reserve for the adult I soon would be.

Meanwhile I was just a slip of a thing, and company for Colm. Colm's mother had been the youngest of Nanny's large family. 'Ten childer,' she would say proudly, 'and all but three of them livin'.' I knew this was meant to impress, but it seemed an indifferent record to me. I felt Nanny would have done better to have been a bit less greedy, and then perhaps sweet Jesus would not have come in the night and snatched the superfluous babies back to sit in the Lord's bosom? Nanny always said that He took the best. Well, looking at Uncle Matt who lived at home unmarried, and Paschal who was simple, you could see He wouldn't have wanted *them* much. Nonetheless, it did seem unfair to have left Nanny such an unsavoury flock and taken the three Wee Angels. I listened with morbid attention to the stories of their deaths, which grew more dramtic and harrowing with every repetition: Roisin, with her saintly nature and her ringlets of raven hair, and her fatal inability to thrive beyond her infancy –

'She just quit growing, God love her! Just wasted clean away. The Lord called her to His keeping.'

'But what was *wrong* with her, Nanny?'

'She was too good for us, my darling. I tell you, the night she died she lay on the couch with her eyes staring wide and Devil the bit she saw us, not even her Mammy that bore her. She was looking towards the throne! Like a feather she was, but you'll never see a lovelier child in Creation. So He called her to His bosom, and her barely three years old . . .'

At this point you could sometimes detect in her voice a definite note of peevishness, but my awed gaze soon dispelled it. To have had this child of God in your house for even three summers was an unregrettable honour. Somehow I had the inherent tact not to try to find out more about what really ailed poor Roisin. Surely doctors had been consulted? But no hole in the heart, no blood disease, no faulty thyroid gland would bring the romantic solace of the picture enshrined in the legend, an unblemished child sacrificed willingly to the glory of the Lord.

In the case of Aidan, diplomacy was even more sorely tested. Aidan was also an angel. He had fallen to his death from the twenty-foot galvanised tin roof overhanging our bottom orchard. There was no given explanation for what he was doing there, and angels do not steal apples, so what was the point of asking? Far better to thrill to the story of how he had hit his head on a boulder in the rocky field – 'mashed his wee brains up like a turnip', as Nanny Magennis put it. I used to prowl furtively round the foot of the wall where the mossy stones protruded from the pasture, and picture, in ghoulish horror, the dead child lying there, his skull split in half and his crimson blood soaking into the grass of the meadow. The image was so vivid that for a year or two I began to see it in my dreams and wake myself by my own screaming. Even so, it was Nanny's third chronicle, the still-born birth of a son, that caused the worst night terrors, and in the actual hearing, made the flesh crawl and the heartbeats pound in the most titillating way.

'And did it hurt much, Nanny?' You knew, of course, it was fearful. You could see Nanny, heaving with agony on the musty sagging bed in the room at the back that smelt of sour milk.

'Hurt, child? May the Holy Mother preserve you from knowing the torment that I endured that night. It took four of them to hoult me down. When the Da went for the doctor he said he could hear the shouts of me every step he took of the way right down to O'Hagan's corner.'

You shuddered, seeing it clearly: the coven of women pinioning the body to the bed, their shadows huge in the guttering light that was all Nanny's oil lamp afforded. And the baby, by dark misfortune unable to find its way to the navel (through which, presumably, normal infants were delivered) bursting horribly through the protesting flesh – 'thon chile had me rent in twain' – and dying before the hour was out, its skin as blue as buttermilk. Yes, that was the picture that haunted me more keenly than all the rest; perhaps partly because Nanny, though she always began it with relish, showed less than her usual confidence as the story ap-

17

proached its end. It was almost as if she was troubled by the fate of this last wee angel. There was less about Jesus's bosom and the glories of the blest. Instead there were curses and mutterings that I could not really follow, and bitter words about lazy priests who preferred to stay at home and warm their backsides before their fires than turn out in the darkness for the draughty purpose of saving souls. This attitude greatly intrigued me. *I* would have kept my reproaches for the doctor who came so late that 'the very mattress was stiff with blood and meself as grey as a corpus'. But with Nanny you knew there were some things you must never ask or say, and discussion about the saving of souls was certainly out of the question; besides, mystery added considerably to the impact of the tale.

I said nothing to my parents about the Magennises' cottage. I had not been forbidden to go there. On the other hand, I knew that this was because it had never crossed their minds that I might do so. They trusted me, and they saw no need to list individual sins if the principle were understood, and here it was unmistakable. They often said that the cottage was no place for a child to be – meaning no place for Colm; it was simply taken for granted that I would know instinctively that it was no place for me.

It had once been the gardener's cottage. Old Magennis had worked for my grandfather, and had always been described to me as an honest, respectable man who remained loyal to the family even during those years in the twenties when houses like Dunvarden were raided for arms in the night, and not infrequently burned to the ground as part of the vicious circle of reprisals that plagued the country in the wake of the Black and Tans. I had doubts about this, for my scepticism had been awakened by Nanny. It was obvious that my parents were completely unable to see through the farcical act of subservience that she put on for their benefit. Poor little Mrs

Magennis, indeed! It irritated me that they should make such a misjudgment, and, beneath the irritation, I was ashamed and frightened at their fallibility. They had got it all wrong – not just Nanny, but their entire impression of Colm's life at the cottage. My mother called it a sin that he had been abandoned there by his own mother and father. Such a place for a child! Those two louts of men, that drunken rascal Matt, and Paschal, dear help him poor creature, as witless as a baby! Just look at the child, a bundle of rags. 'I hope you speak civilly if you see him at the bus stop,' my father would say sternly, and tell me again for the hundredth time how Colm's father Pat, Wee Patsy Hourican, as he was called, had worked down at McMurtry's for the last forty years, and had joined the firm on the very selfsame day as my father himself had come back from the war to take up the family business – 'and a decent wee man he has always been, never mind he kicks with his left. If there were a few more like him, we'd have a sight less trouble'. In those bright days of the sixties, my father took a great pride in the lack of discrimination that he showed when recruiting his work force. It was not his fault unemployment was so high in Killycreel, and nor could he help it if ninety percent of the unemployed were Catholics: he gave jobs according to merit, he said, and of course it was well known that few Catholics were as diligent or reliable as Protestants. All the same, since Protestant applicants were outnumbered by five to one, he not infrequently hired a Taig, a Fenian, a Holy Roman, for want of a better alternative. Years later he said to me that at that time around a third of his unskilled labour was Nationalist, could I call that discrimination? No other Loyalist firm could boast of such magnanimity. What had happened was not his doing. Everyone knew that McMurtry's was the mainstay of Killycreel.

And Killycreel needed a mainstay; its whole rigging was in tatters. The drab streets that led to the river, the stagnant

19

canal, the abandoned warehouses, the empty quaysides, the warren of tumbledown houses on the hill all emanated a hopeless air of dejection that contrasted almost absurdly with the beauty of its setting. As a child you observed this phenomenon without question or surprise. You accepted the length of the dole queue, and the fact that the fine new bypass that was planned to skirt the town centre had simply petered away and ended in a rubbish tip that bottlenecked the traffic. You did not seek reasons to explain why the people from the Old Town were regarded as inferior by those who had escaped from it. Rusty cranes still lined the horizon, but you did not ask anyone why the lock-gates rotted on the canals and the stockyards lay deserted. Yet the atmosphere was your element, absorbed into your soul with the stories of Nanny Magennis and the acrid smell of her cottage, with the stench of cat in the little shed at the back of O'Hagan's pub where you and Colm left your bikes and parted as if you were strangers, so that he could catch the Catholic, and you the Protestant bus. It was in your bones, as much part of you as the bigotry you were born to, that you were unconscious of learning, that made my father see the often-used phrase 'he's a decent man for all that he's a Catholic' as a true expression of tolerance and liberality, rather than a staggering insult to a third of the population. And indeed, to voice this opinion *did* make him a tolerant man in comparison with his associates. To defend a Catholic takes courage, the moral courage that does not flinch from alienating friends on whose goodwill and support you depend for your safety and your livelihood.

In the end, his efforts to run his firm on integrated lines had foundered when violence broke out again in the latter years of the sixties. McMurtry's had had their share of it, with a couple of lorries mobbed and a fire bomb or two in the timber yards, and the Protestant workers in fury had

turned against the minority, claiming that the IRA had infil-
trated the premises through its Roman Catholic employees.
A few suspects were instantly hounded out, and others drifted away, fearful of intimidation in the new and hostile atmosphere. Though it greatly distressed my father, McMurtry's
acquired a name for being a Loyalist stronghold, and soon
Catholics ceased to apply for jobs in the coal and timber
yards for fear of the other workers. Increasingly outnumbered, a few old hands stayed on and were grudgingly accepted until they reached retirement. Pat Hourican was among
the last of this steadily dwindling band and remained, as he
had always been, a favourite with my father, who remembered him with affection as a cocky strip of a lad with the
impudence of a monkey and a glad eye for the ladies. He
seemed to be smaller than ever these days, but was jaunty
still, and spry, with his flat cap stuck on the back of his head
and his trousers rolled up at the bottom. When a bad chest
put paid to the humping of coal, my father had fitted him in
on the rota of ageing employees who manned the little watch-
man's booth that stood beside the security gates in the high
perimeter fence around the storage depot.

He had been on duty there last week on the night when the
fire began, and had later been found unconscious halfway
between his own cabin, which housed the untouched alarm
controls, and the small pedestrian door that he had presumably opened under some misapprehension. At least that was
what I understood on hearing about it from Jim. At the time
I had been more interested in news about my father, who had
stayed at the office working late, as he very frequently did,
and was caught by the blast as he passed the side of the
warehouse to reach the car park. He had been flung quite a
distance and had fallen, striking his head and cracking his
ribs on the bonnet of one of the stationary lorries. He was
suffering from concussion and shock, but as Jim correctly

said, he was lucky to be alive at all: had it not been for the efficiency of the fire brigade and the Army, he could well have burned to death.

As it was, he and Pat went to hospital, lying side by side in the ambulance, two victims of an ancient feud so relentless and so deep that there was no hope of placating it by their own lifetime of friendship. And it had been friendship, surely? At all events, I knew that my father was genuinely fond of Pat, his longest-serving employee. For him, the special relationship that was born on that first day they had shared at the yards had survived, and allowed for a ritual banter between them which afforded him much amusement. 'He's a caution, that Wee Pat. You'd never credit the cheek of him . . .' But the cheek, and the liking behind it, had become an established feature of his every working day; just as once, long ago, my own daily routine had relied on the presence of Colm. Now, as I drove over the cattle grid at the back gate of Dunvarden, and felt through the comfortable seat of my car the bone-shaking rumble and jar that had once rattled through my bicycle wheels, I was brought sharply back to the childhood in which Colm had figured so largely.

Once Jimmy had left Killycreel and gone to board at Campbell, in effect I became an only child. Although Jim was never unkind to me, he had no inclination to play with a sister so much younger, and besides he was much too busy. He joined the local football club, he enrolled in the Boy's Brigade, he camped with the Combined Cadet Force, he sailed with the nearby yacht club, and I worshipped him from a distance. He was big and tough and tall; a gregarious soul, always one of the boys: good at games, rowdy, cheerful, popular. He had a fund of terrible jokes with which he amused his friends, and although he was certainly very far from becoming an intellectual, it was plain that his contemporaries considered him no fool, and that he was shrewd enough in his way, beneath the hearty manner. My mother, with total lack of success, attempted to modify his accent and his bearing to her own genteel requirements, but accepted her failure equably: he was a bonny son, and McMurtry men, though crudely hewn, were diamonds right through to the centre; if she wanted to polish and refine, her chance would come with me. Men were men, and women were women to her, and a certain degree of earthiness was part of masculinity. If her husband and her boy were a bit on the rough-and-ready side she might scold, but at heart she was proud of it. Besides, Jim would go into the business and live in Killycreel where everyone knew that he was the son of an old and respected family. Girls' fortunes were much more fluid. Girls could marry anyone. And it would be nice if Alison did well for herself and felt comfortable in the houses and the company of those rarefied Englishy few where she herself felt so ill at ease, unsophisticated and provincial. She envied them in spite of herself, and in spite of all the fun that Carson and Jimmy were wont to poke at their high-falutin voices . . . So, ironically, my mother, who was to suffer more than anyone else in the family from my changed attitudes and opinions, spent busy years devising the route to the breach ahead while I played on the moor with Colm through the long empty weeks of the holidays, or met him in the term-time by the drunken dolmen stone in the hedge below Nanny's cottage, for the ride to O'Hagan's corner.

Both of us were happy children; I was unconditionally so, having no idea what was in store for me. Colm's sky was occasionally clouded by the periodic efforts of his parents to make him come home. He was Wee Pat's last and seventh child, and his mother had nearly died of him as Nanny disgustedly put it. I was never sure whether her scorn was aroused by her daughter's weakness in performing a natural function, or by her perverse refusal to die and add one story more to the list of family tragedies. Still, the illness had been dramatic, and when she came out of hospital Nanny took the baby home to give her daughter a bit of peace from his constant demands for attention. 'For were you the twisted wee article, Colm? Ye had us all walkin' the floor from the sun went down till it riz again!' – this was said with great pride and affection. Colm's babyhood was obviously a precious memory to everyone at the cottage. Paschal giggled and grinned at the thought of it (though admittedly, faced with direct appeal, Paschal always giggled and grinned), and even dour Uncle Matt, lost somewhere beneath the stubble that grew dense and forbidding before the week's end and was only removed for Mass, could be seen to smile if you knew where to look, and nodded his head in agreement. There was no lack of love at Nanny's, and on love Colm cheerfully throve, finding it an adequate supplement to a diet of boiled potatoes, and a more than satisfactory swap for hot water and clean clothes, electric light and a lavatory and a household of virtual strangers. I could always tell immediately when another attempt had been made to take him away from Nanny's. He would be there, waiting for me ostensibly as normal, beside the dolmen stone. But one look and you knew it had happened; he had simply shrunk, deflated, no longer a wiry little boy in comfortable grubby clothes but a ragged starving monkey, undersized, neglected, filthy. Confidence had accounted for half his bulk, for his cheeky simian smile, for the muscle in his rickety limbs and the warmth of his vitality. Dread had squeezed him as dry as a mummy.

'Did they come for you again?' He nodded, not looking at me. They always came on Sundays. Wee Pat had a brother whose friend had a car they would borrow after Mass, a huge banging heap of metal much the same size as the cottage. Sometimes coming back from church ourselves, we would happen upon the thing as it ground and belched its way up the hill, weighed down by uncountable Houricans, its underside scraping the ridge of grass in the middle of the road, its exhaust pipe bouncing up and down and throwing out sparks like a bonfire. The look of it gave me the shivers. I had no possible way of knowing if it meant a kidnap attempt or a routine Sunday visit, for each Sunday one of her children collected Nanny for Mass, and another brought her back again with Colm squeezed in beside her. Matt and Paschal, like two outriders, fresh shaved in their Sunday best, flanked the motor car on their bicycles. In comparison with these outings, the abduction attempts were a rarity: Nanny's wrath was not a thing that anyone in their senses would court without good reason. But the reasons were growing more numerous. This time, it seemed Nanny was ill; not well enough, it was put to Colm, to be bothered with rearing a youngster. It was too much for her at her time of life. No matter what she said, it was best he returned to his father's house where he could be properly cared for.

'But what would she do without you?'

Colm shrugged. It appeared Nanny too had been reduced to asking this, weak enough to resort to pleading instead of showing them the door and bawling them down the road as she usually did at such moments. This had left Colm very shaken. Despite the spectacular crises that were commonplace in his life, and the drama and the ritual attendant on every deathbed, it had not occurred to him before that Nanny herself could fall ill, and moreover was not immortal. It had not occurred to me either. Nanny seemed as timeless as the moor, as the hills, as the dolmen stone, too ancient to think of as ageing. All at once it was horribly plain that this was not the case at all.

'Nanny's auld,' Colm's voice was savage. 'When you're auld ye get sick more often. You're not fit till mind the house

25

no more, that's what me Da told me. When you're auld, you get very very sick because your time's near over, and then . . .' I could see this was leading straight to the Bosom of the Lord, and that it had got to be stopped at once.

'Ach now, away with you Colm! Don't say them things about your Nan. You know there's nothing wrong but what a bit of rest won't cure. Sure, Matt's away picking potatoes, and you can look after yourself anyroads. Why don't you call out the doctor? He'd give her some medicine to make her well.'

Colm stubbornly shook his head. He was terrified of doctors. Doctors took people off to hospital and kept them until they were dead, or they got in touch with the Welfare, who removed you by force and saw to it you had no chance to slip back again. In a recent moment of stress, Wee Pat had used the Welfare as a threat to get Colm home with him, though we all knew the threat to be empty; no one sullied their good name by asking strangers to come in and deal with their family problems. I dropped the idea of the doctor. But Colm was lost in thought, intrigued with the notion of medicines. That was clearly what Nanny needed.

'Have ye any medicine up at the house?'

Of course! The very thing! I looked at Colm admiringly: he always came up with an answer. We had a whole cupboard of bottles and pills dating back to goodness knows when, all jumbled up and forgotten about, but with names and dates on the labels.

After school I made a selection of these and tiptoed out through the hall, my satchel fat with their magic. I carried them with pride down the back lane to the cottage and handed them over to Colm, who, with something amounting to reverence, wiped the oilskin tablecloth clean with the flat of his sleeve, to receive them. It was hard to make out the instructions, for the chemist had written them all in a hand

26

that was faded and spidery, but an excellent memory helped me. I recognised the jar of pills left behind by my own Gran who had something wrong with her waterworks, and the tiny ones that poor Grandpa used to take before he died, to stop him having heart attacks. We both agreed these would be suitable as the patients were all of a similar age. On the symptomatic side, since Nanny was racked by a rattling cough and was suddenly burning with fever, we decided upon a bottle I had had when I was five and had been very hot with the measles; this had thickened and smelled disgusting, so we added some cough elixir and Paschal declared it was fine. Then we took the lot through to Nanny.

Colm had told me she was poorly, much worse than she had been yesterday when checked by the family, but I still was shocked by what I saw. She really looked very frightening. Vertical, her face had hollows enough, but lying there in the bed, all her features seemed to have fallen in. Her eyes had vanished completely beneath the skull-like jut of her brows. Her mouth was just a hole. There were caverns where her cheeks should have been. Worse still, when we nervously roused her, she did not argue or grumble or curse, but let Colm support her head while I doled out the pills and the syrup and gave her sips of water, most of which ran in rivulets down her chin and on to her skinny chest.

I could see we were only just in time: Nanny needed the medicine badly. I felt a disloyal longing to hurry home and tell, just to lift the responsibility. But I knew that any adult, perhaps even Uncle Matthew, would call the doctor in, and that would be an end of us – Nanny off to die in hospital, and Colm away to his father's house in the Old Town of Killycreel where I would never see him again. No, the price of relief was too heavy. Rather we must thank our lucky stars that Uncle Matt was away, lifting maincrop spuds and sleeping rough on the other side of the mountains, and would not be back to interfere. Colm would be left all alone, for nobody could count Paschal, and I myself must soon be gone to get ready for my tea, a large cooked meal which our family ate when my father returned from the office. I could not miss tea without everyone coming out to look for me and panicking if I could not be found, and that would lead to discovery.

I fidgeted, starting to distance myself from the body on the bed and the anguished face beside it. I loved them, but something stronger than love made me want to get away, away from the wild look in Colm's eyes and from Nanny's horrible breathing, away from the nagging feeling that more needed to be done about the situation, despite the cost in freedom. I wanted my mother and father. I wanted normality. I ran all the way home from the cottage. I ate my pork chop with relish. I followed my mother around the house and chattered ceaselessly of anything that came into my head. I played dominoes with my father. I spent ages fooling around in my bath. But in the end there came a moment when I could no longer put off the evil hour of my bedtime and I could not pretend to myself any more that I was not deeply afraid.

The night that Nanny nearly died. That is how I still think about it, though there cannot have been much wrong with her. Indeed to judge by the way she survived our amateur doctoring, her strength must have been prodigious. I expect she just had a feverish cold; but I thought I had left her to die, and Colm to watch her doing it. And what made it all much more dreadful was that I was unable to make myself leave the sanctuary of my bed and creep down the dark stairs and the darker hall and the night-black lane to the cottage, and join Colm in his vigil. I had my torch by my side and I knew quite well what I ought to do. I simply could not do it. Terror literally paralysed me. I hardly dared move in bed, let alone step out of it into the maw of the nightmare I had created. I felt as if I was awake all night, though I probably slept quite well, as most

28

children do at the worst of times. I certainly slept through the dawn (the hour when I had promised myself a compromise visit to Colm), for I woke to a stricken morning, bright with sun, lively with birdsong, and poisoned with guilt and foreboding.

I was sick in the middle of breakfast. My mother, already disturbed by my gloom, insisted I go back to bed, saying maybe I was catching the 'flu, and a day off school wouldn't harm me. But bed was now a tormented place, and after an hour or two I begged to go out in the healthy air which all grown-ups spoke of so highly as an antidote to illness. I forced myself down the lane with my heart wedged into my stomach and thumping away like a butterchurn.

In the backyard of her cottage I found Nanny feeding the hens, without much vivacity, it is true; her 'Chuckie, chuckie, chuckie!' lacked its usual piercing quality, and the grain did not fly from her hand like the pellets from a shotgun as it did on ordinary mornings: nonetheless, she was feeding the chickens, and you do not do that if you're dead. I burst into tears at the sight of her.

She took me inside the cottage, but even when we were sitting one on either side of the range and I had been given a biscuit, I could not control my weeping. 'Whisht Alison, what ails ye, child?' and 'Quit now, there's a pet!' and 'Mother of God, are ye bereft?' alike failed to compose me. It was not until Nanny picked up two pills that Colm had put by her chair and swallowed them down with a draught of tea, that I felt a flicker of comfort. At least I had provided the pills, and, although when compared with the shame of leaving Colm alone all night because I was a coward, it was not very much to be proud of, it did help my tears to dry and enable me to tell Nanny that I was off school with a fever, and would she tell this to her grandson?

On the surface, face was saved, and, as Nanny was better, no harm was done – yet nothing seemed the same, for my comprehension of trouble had taken a huge leap forward. Perched there on Nanny's rocking chair, I was still too young to assess that what I had learned was the power of fear, and how that power can hold sway over all our better intentions, even to the betrayal of friendship; but I writhed with the pain of bad conscience, and the guilt and remorse remained.

Dunvarden House stands on rising ground nearly two miles back from the main road, with the empty moor behind it, and an unbroken view of the mountains where they meet the sea at the end of the Killycreel valley. When I first went to school in England, the image of this view quite literally haunted me. I had only to shut my eyes, and the moutains were there, curving downwards to the water that lay between them. The picture, when it first came to me, was always in monochrome, a two-dimensional imprint silhouetted against the eyelids like the stark impression left behind when you stare at something bright, so bright that it hurts, and then turn away. Homesickness could furnish the skeleton with all its remembered complexions, the ominous navy-blue of stormy days, the silver of dawn, the gaudy purple of heather, the extravagance of sunset – but that was wallowing deliberately in sentiment and I soon learned to control it. Warding off the initial vision was a very different thing; it appeared without any warning, and even now can startle me. The mountains simply materialise, their outline is stamped on the brain as unwanted and immovable as any other birthmark.

Tonight, as I got out of the car, the low ceiling of mist and rain had blanked them out completely, yet I was acutely aware of them, blacker than the surrounding blackness, with the lighthouse flashing between them as you see it on cloudless nights, and the sea as smooth as a summer lake, milkpale with reflected moonlight. For an instant this was quite real to me, recreated by my mind and neatly furnished from memory to fit the picture demanded of it. And with it, sharp and immediate and still as bitter as gall, the atmosphere of a hundred other homecomings came back to me: the pleasure soured with resentment; the words that could not be said for the sake of pride; the knowledge, ugly, frightening, yet growing strongly, that the exile of my schooling meant that loving Killycreel could never again be the easy and uncomplicated emotion I had thought to enjoy for a lifetime.

I turned towards the house, where the porch light already shone out in the dusk as a sign of the prodigal's welcome, and as I reached for the handle, my mother opened the door with such jack-in-the-box precision that we came together abruptly, almost bumping into each other. The expression of pained relief (for my late but safe arrival) and of dutiful goodwill (a daughter is always a daughter) was wiped suddenly from her face by a rush of genuine delight at seeing me there on the doorstep. My own defensive attitude (I came as soon as I could, but I happen to have obligations too – child, job, the man I live with) vanished in my immediate response to it. We embraced impulsively, both close to tears. My mother feels so slight when you put your arms round her that it is easy to forget how amazingly tough and strong she has always been, both physically and in terms of her own principles. No arguments shake her opinions, her moral precepts survive all assaults that life makes upon them without showing the slightest weakening. As it functions for her body, the immune system in her mind casts out all injurious doubts and fears and keeps the system as healthy as it can be, given her feelings for me. In a world where all shades of grey have been remorselessly swept aside by the blacks and whites of conviction, I cause mortifying confusion. I am her Achilles' heel, the one point where misgiving can enter and threaten her sense of values, causing ripples of uncertainty in the calm of a soul born again.

Naturally, this situation causes her resentment and anger. She is ashamed that her love for me is stronger than the will to renounce me in public by righteous condemnation of my lifestyle. But she cannot condone it either. She takes a middle road which involves us in tortuous word-games built round her resolution to ignore Benjamin's existence. As I have been living with him for nearly ten years, I am equally determined not to deny him, and to speak about him openly. I laugh about this with Ben, but I seldom find it funny when I am with my mother. Instead I am irritated and hurt by the farcical obstinacy with which she pursues her attack upon me. This is harder to understand in the light of her final acceptance of Adam as my husband – but perhaps her instinctive compassion during Adam's illness and death seems in retrospect merely a weakness to her, a battle lost to the Devil? Or just a battle lost to me? This good moment was one of the few when such matters were shelved between us. On a full emotional tide of love and concern for my father, we were wholeheartedly united. Our embrace acknowledged our thoughts of him, our awareness that he could have died, our shared shock, shared relief and shared sorrow that he, who was so gentle, should have been the target of violence.

'You'll have been in to see him today?'

She nodded. 'He's coming on nicely. Please God, he'll be out Saturday. He'll be better at home. It depresses him, being stuck in that place all day with nothing to do to pass the time. You know how your father worries. And the nights are the worst. By himself all night!'

It occurred to me suddenly that in forty years they had scarcely spent a night apart from each other; that she never had slept in an empty house. I looked at her anxiously, and guilt made my voice sharp. 'Why did you stay here? You could have gone down to Jimmy's.' She was always in and out of Jim's home, and did she not frequently say that

Heather was like a daughter to her, meaning that she was some compensation for all that I had failed to be?

'No doubt I could,' she said, and added thoughtfully, half to herself, 'I suppose I didn't want to – not with Carson in there on his lonesome. It wouldn't have seemed right. He might have felt I was siding with Jim because of what had happened.' She paused, and then said in her usual voice, 'No. The firm's the men's affair. Home's home, and work's work, and best kept apart.' This last phrase was one of her favourites, often used to show disapproval of my working happily as a picture expert and valuer for one of the big London salerooms instead of marrying again and making a home for my son with the single-minded devotion she had given to Dunvarden. But today the remark was mechanical. Conflict between Father and Jim, so long confined to the office and viewed almost with indulgence (a wee bit impetuous sometimes, but a stouthearted laddie, our Jim), had clearly encroached on areas where its presence was once unimaginable. For my mother, whose pride was enormous, to admit as much to me, must mean things were very bad indeed, and dismay silenced me for a moment. 'What new scheme is Jimmy hatching, then?' I said at last, treading with care. If I treated her words too seriously, she would wish she had never spoken them.

As it was, she was slow to answer me. She was laying a tray for tea with paper napkins and fine china cups, and a chocolate cake on a doily. This meal, with dinner to follow, had replaced the huge high tea we had eaten when we were children, and I knew she thought it more stylish, more in keeping with what I was used to now. She kept her back turned to me and when she spoke I could tell that she was struggling to hold her voice steady.

'Jim's not himself these days, Alison. He wants some contract through that Daddy won't countenance at all – and this

33

is not the first time. I don't know the ins and outs of it. It's some political thing.' She knew of course what the contract was, but I did not interrupt her. My mother has always pretended that she does not know anything about business affairs in general and our own business in particular, this being the province of menfolk. 'The bomb at the works – Jim says it wouldn't have happened to us at all if Daddy had done what he asked him. Well, that's as may be. I'm no judge of that,' (she agreed with Jim here, I could see) 'but I will not stand for trickery, nor for anyone cheating your father. His own son to take advantage, when he was so shocked and ill that he didn't know what he was doing!'

She whisked up the tray laid for tea, and carried it through to the sitting-room. 'The impudence of him!' she said. 'I wouldn't have believed it! He turned up the very next day to see your father in hospital with a letter of power of attorney, all made out by the solicitors. "Just you sign this, Pop," he says, "so I can look after everything until you're on your feet again." And your father barely conscious, lying there too confused to know if he was badly hurt or not, maybe thinking he was dying!

'Well, I was sitting beside him, and I took the paper from Jim, and I tore it up in front of his face and dropped it into the basket. "You'll be pleased to know that we won't need this," I said, and I smiled at him in case poor Daddy could see me, "for your father'll be fine in a day or two, and you can bring documents in to him if he needs to put his name to anything of importance." So . . .' She held out my cup of tea and the light of achievement died out of her face, 'So that's the way it is, Alison. I could hardly go down to Jim's and behave as though nothing had happened, not when I had caught him red-handed. If he'd got his power of attorney, he'd have had that contract away and into the post like a streak of light, and dear knows what else besides it. And all because Daddy was too sick to know that he was signing away the authority to run the works according to his principles. He's a good man, is your father. Maybe too good for these times.'

'Is that what Jim says?'

She shook her head. 'To Jimmy, it's just weakness, and weakness has never seemed good to him. Oh, he loves your father all right. He tells himself that Pop's getting old, that his grasp of affairs is going, and that it's his duty to save the firm.'

'You know that's not true,' I said, 'and Jim knows it too. It's just an excuse. The whole thing is political. They'd have been at loggerheads years ago, only that's not Daddy's way. Jim's a bigot, an extremist.'

Her lips tightened with displeasure. 'I'll not hear that said of Jimmy. To you, any Christian soul is a bigot, if he upholds his faith against Popery and terrorism . . .'

'They are not the same thing, Mother.'

'Indeed? Well, it's very kind of you to put me right on that. Of course you would know all about it, living somewhere else entirely.' Her voice had grown flat as Jim's with the effort of her sarcasm.

Stung by it, I said unwisely, 'And where is Daddy living, then?'

'Don't drag your father in to support your views,' she said hotly. 'Your father is a Christian. He's a God-fearing man. And if sometimes he trusts the other side more than is wise, its because, in his faith, he cannot conceive of human folk being so wicked. And not because . . .' Here she stopped with a gasp, and I knew she had started to say 'not because he's an unbeliever like you, who has turned from the path of righteousness'.

Once I would have finished the sentence for her, in the mocking and insolent tone of one who has heard it all before, and this would have roused her anger to the point where it

35

would have possessed us both. Harsh words would have flown between us, as painful as we could make them, but now I sat speechlessly, staring into my cup and striving to keep some measure of detachment. If I could stand back a little, then perhaps I would not be so hurt and enraged by my mother. I would focus objectively, and feel no need to justify myself against her criticism, which does me no harm whatever. I would look at her and see – what would I see? I risked a glance towards where she sat by the fireside, rigid with reproach and defiance, prepared to be torn in two by her duty to profess the Word and her love for the lost soul who turned from it, and I knew I was looking at someone as incapable of guile or treachery as of any form of reasoned debate or compromise. Brave, honest and doggedly obstinate. Devoted, but not very bright. She would gladly have died to defend home and faith, but where home and faith were divided within or against each other, the guidelines of her life became frighteningly tangled. Her convictions now lay with Jim, but her loyalty to her husband was confusing her response to them. Jim was Saved, while his father remained in the dark. How was it then that Jim could attempt to wrest power from him in a way that was barely honest? Did the ends indeed justify the means, and if so, must she try to view Father's goodness through Jim's relentless eyes and see it as a weakness? Or would that be betrayal of Carson? In either case, what should she do to keep father and son united? For the first time in my life, I was seeing her totally at a loss in a family situation that was not centred on my own shortcomings, and I was ashamed to find myself subject to a nasty twinge of spite and satisfaction. Trusting all black sheep were a prey to this, I held grimly on to my silence until the malice had drained from it, and been replaced by pity and the bleak inadequacy of not knowing what to say in a hopeless situation that concerns someone you care for.

But at least the long pause seemed to serve as a truce. As I groped for words of comfort, my mother suggested civilly that I drink up my tea. 'You could go straight down and see Daddy – I know he'll be waiting for you. And if you're quick about it, you'll get a wee while with him before Jimmy calls in with his business talk on his way home from the office.'

'Don't you want to come down with me?'

She sniffed disparagingly. 'No – you go on, dear. I've seen him today. I'll stay here and put my feet up.' The words, innocuous in themselves, were transfigured by her tone till they carried the old familiar charge 'I know when I'm not wanted' that had sounded throughout my childhood. I knew better than to contest an implication of sacrifice that would only grow stronger when challenged. My mother enjoys feeling martyred. When I left, she would hurry away to prepare a complicated meal that neither of us needed, and thanks and compliments alike would be met with a tight-lipped smile designed to show that she knew her place as Martha to my Mary, and that she accepted it selflessly despite her fatigue and the pain of knowing what a happy time we had all enjoyed without her.

I got up, reassured by this evidence that we still had not reached a crisis. When faced with real disaster, my mother throws off the complex as a child might abandon a toy, and behaves with a true unselfishness that asks for no recognition. Her wish to feel mildly put-upon was like a guarantee that life would go on as usual, and for once I felt almost eager to take the part of the thoughtless child that had been allotted to me ever since I could remember – nothing untoward could happen so long as we played our familiar roles. Yet as I went into the hall with the heartless 'See you later' that the thoughtless child's exit demanded, I was glad to see the lights of a car sweeping round in front of the house, and to know

37

I would not be leaving her alone with her feelings of grievance. Some company would cheer her up.

I opened the inner door as her visitor opened the outer one, and I saw a burly figure silhouetted against the outside light and appearing to fill the porch in a faintly menacing manner, as though he might burst out of it. He was wearing a plain dark overcoat of a kind that is to be found in its tens of thousands in London, but is rare in Northern Ireland where it often denotes an Englishman or a member of the cloth. Now the man as much as the overcoat told me this was a pastoral visit. Despite the self-effacing bob with which he slid into the hall, he radiated complacency. As he saw who I was he stepped backwards, holding out both hands, palm upwards, in a gesture half of surprise and half of benediction, and after a couple of seconds during which he made clear he could hardly believe the evidence of his eyes, broke out 'If it isn't Alison, come back to help her Mammy! May the Lord be praised!' He held his pose and nodded thoughtfully, as though marvelling on the grace of God and His power to call forth some virtue even in the worst of sinners. Although there was little trace of the Brian Burns I remembered in the sanctimonious manner or the heavy form before me, I recognised his face – or rather the little grouping of unprepossessing features that appreared to have been transplanted from the face I once had known to the centre of a much larger one, into which they were rapidly sinking.

I had not seen Brian for twenty years, and I knew it was foolish of me to dislike the man for the schoolboy's faults, or to pick up the accusation that I was neglecting my parents, implied in his greeting to me. Yet I felt raw with irritation. It was all I could do to shake hands with him, to show him in to my mother and watch the flattering way she jumped up from her chair to receive him, pink and flustered with gratification. 'Why, Brian! You shouldn't have bothered!' Still smiling, she turned to me. 'Brian's church is up in the City now, and such wonderful comfort he gives us. He speaks out for us all, in the name of the Lord. He's quite a celebrity – always getting into the papers!' She laid a hand on her visitor's arm. 'But you don't forget us, Brian. You don't forget Killycreel. Old friends were ever the best friends, and where would we be without them? We all look to our friendships to get us through times like these.'

'And to God's love, Mrs McMurtry. To God's love. There lies our solace.' He allowed a moment for pious thought, and then went on graciously. 'But I've just been with your husband. Sad I was to hear of his trouble. Ah yes . . .' – here his manner grew suddenly stern – 'Ah yes, I was sad indeed! Yet the ways of the Lord are manifold. Perhaps He has ordained it that this very trouble will act as a sign to a soul that has gone astray – a good soul and a worthy soul, but one who has lost direction, has strayed from the pathway of the Lord through reluctance to challenge the sin in the bosoms of those around him?' His voice sank dramatically, and then swelled again with the cadence of the preacher in the pulpit, and he shook one finger for emphasis.

As I opened my mouth to say 'You mean in the bosoms of Catholics?', I saw my mother stiffen, every form of apprehension was written on her face: apprehension of insult to her guest, of her daughter's disgrace in the process, of her own invidious standing as one who had reared a child that had failed in its allegiance (those not with us are against us), and of having the simple pleasure of this visit snatched away before she could start to enjoy it. I swallowed back the sentence. Brian Burns was beyond all argument, he would simply relish the chance to attack apostasy face to face in front of one of his faithful, and my mother had had enough to bear. 'I'd better get on,' I said. 'I was just going down to the hospital.'

'Yes, your Daddy said he was expecting you.' Brian

managed to sound avuncular, a very much older man speaking to an adolescent. He turned back to my mother. 'Dear me, poor Mr McMurtry! It's hard for him to realise that his pride has led him to such a pass! But we prayed a while together. Every hill and mountain shall be laid low.'

I slammed the door behind me. In the matter of levelling mountains, I felt Brian had further to go than when he was dancing attendance on the bullies of Killycreel Grammar School. Or perhaps, since he had started life as a sycophant and a cheat, he saw himself now as a valley miraculously exalted? I would have liked to choke him. As I struggled into my coat I could hear his public voice again, beginning to pray with my mother. 'Oh Lord, let us make our lives in Thee, and not fall into the mire of heresy and damnation!' Nowhere else could the words have sounded the same, 'Thee' was bellowed, 'damnation' chanted on a querulous upward singsong that carried no meaning at all, but that caught me unexpectedly with a stab of absurd nostalgia: all those Sundays I'd sat with my parents, prim and well-behaved as could be except for the odd kick at Jimmy that no one ever noticed, and had heard this same intonation, loud and soft like the wind in the trees, with the stress placed as if by a maniac on words quite unsuited to emphasis. 'Horror HATH taken hold UPON me, for I have forsaken thy LAW.' Only then there was no horror, there was nothing but warmth and security, roast potatoes at home in the oven and Colm to play with till tea and heaven at the end of it all. Did Brian still look to that heaven, confident that by vilifying all other beliefs than his own, and consigning those who held them to eternities of torment, he had made his own place there a certainty? I would have liked to say no, but I knew that was just what he did believe. And if he should feel himself called to defend the saved and the Saviour's name by expressions of solidarity that required the violent repression of what he saw as sin (and with the sin, the sinner), he would do so with the same relish that he used to show as a child when abusing the weak or outnumbered – only now the relish was holy, the violence sanctified, and the guilt rationalised to extinction by the zeal of the crusader marching virtuously under his banner, I CAME NOT TO SEND PEACE, BUT A SWORD.

I tried to put Brian behind me as I drove down to the hospital, but I was too jarred by the meeting, and by the vigorous way my memories of him had survived the years since I last had seen him. It was hard to put these in sequence: except that I was thirteen when I went to school in England, nothing of significance dated them. We did not move house, no one close to me died, each Christmas was much the same as the Christmas before, birthdays came and went. Well fed, I grew gradually taller than Colm on his potatoes. At some moment, I passed casually from the fee-paying prep department into Killycreel Grammar School proper, an event that I hardly remember since continuity between the two was completely maintained from the same friends to the same uniform, and for prosperous middle-class children the eleven-plus exam, known to us as the qualifying, was not a traumatic experience. If you failed, your parents could pay for a place, and in any case most of you, with the help of small classes and literate homes, were exceedingly likely to pass it – and, as expected, I did so. Equally predictably, from his back-row seat in a crowded form and homework tossed off in a cottage where the only book was the breviary and Nanny the one source of aid, Colm failed and went on to St Christopher's, where his quick wits and latent abilities were shortly to die of discouragement. Neither of us considered this strange or worthy of any attention, although we both acknowledged that Colm was the leader. Colm thought up the better games, evaded trouble more cunningly, told the most exciting stories,

41

had a formidable memory for legend and for song, and could play airs on the harmonica without the advantage of lessons. When he ran out of tunes he composed them – a jig here, a come-all-ye there, derivative of the ceilidh, and occasionally made excursions into pieces inspired by the organist on his weekly visits to Mass, or by hymns heard at school assembly. The look of Colm's mouth-organ, a battered insanitary instrument of chipped wood and rusty tin, with the chrome and the paint so worn away that you could not tell red from silver, was suddenly as plain to me as if it was in my hand, brought back from oblivion by Brian Burns who once had tried to plunder it, and for the first time had forced me to declare against My Own in a public way, in a public place.

I remember that it was summer. And it must have been the last summer of all, because I had started to go to piano lessons in Killycreel once a week when school was over, thus missing the usual school bus. That particular afternoon, Colm had been kept in and had missed it too. Streetwise, we ignored each other while we waited for the next one, and perched ourselves speechlessly at opposite ends of the dirty bench between the canal and the roadway. We had always been perfectly conscious that our friendship was not a thing to be exposed to the world at large. Our different social backgrounds would not have mattered much at this stage among our contemporaries had we been of the same religion and both gone to Killycreel Grammar School, but the sort of companionship we shared could only have been seen as an act of blatant perversity in view of our different persuasions. Catholic schoolboys and Protestant schoolgirls, as neighbours, could reasonably be on terms of nodding acquaintanceship and speak to each other politely, but intimacy was out of line – though until that summer day, this had given me no food for thought. It was simply part of life's pattern and second nature to both of us; there was no disloyalty in

42

pretending detachment from Colm, since it was clearly expedient. So we sat in the warmth of the late afternoon and waited contentedly, with the day's gossip held in abeyance, and our shoulders turned slightly outwards to show we had met by chance only and were travelling separately.

It was early closing in Killycreel, and the schools had gone home an hour ago. There was no one else at the bus stop. The pavements along the Mall were as empty as the canal itself, and after a little while Colm fished out his harmonica and struck up a tune to pass the time. I can still recall the very bars of the jig he had started to play at the moment when I caught sight of the boys emerging from one of the alleyways and beginning to stroll towards us across the empty road. I can still see the green wire litter bin with the swarm of flies around it, and the newspaper screw of fish and chips on which I fixed my stare, as though blotting them out might make them go, for I knew by some basic instinct that they were coming for Colm, and worse than that I knew that this had to mean they were coming for me. The jig died: Colm, too, had seen them. I continued to gaze at the litter bin until a black school shoe came into my vision and crushed the wasps and the rotting plum they fed on, and all hope of escape was over. I looked up. They were big lads by then, Dick Bond, Joe Baker and Brian Burns, and their reputation was awesome. Dick and Joe were known as the Heavies, and respected in their way, if only for their muscle power and the dominance it brought them, but Brian Burns was both hated and feared; he was tall and weedy then, slower to fill out than the other two, but with more brains than both put together. Dick and Joe might actually carry out the raids on little boys outside McGuigan's sweet shop, or wreck stolen bikes on joy rides, or torture chosen victims, but it was Brian Burns who devised the elaborate system of intimidation and blackmail that prevented complaints

43

against them. This had never affected me, for they seldom turned their attention to girls unless one should presume to challenge them, and my charity had not aspired to that. Like all my family, I knew very well when to safeguard myself by keeping a low profile. No McMurtry runs out to meet trouble, he lets it come to him and hopes it will get side-tracked towards someone else on its journey. But this time the opportunity to look the other way, which was perfectly open to me, had abruptly lost its attraction.

I stood up and turned towards Colm. They were gathered round him now, Dick and Joe on each side, Brian out in front well clear of possible injury, and for an instant I saw him as he would appear in their eyes, an intolerably cheeky urchin, dirty, ruffianly, disrespectful, just asking for a lesson from the rulers of Killycreel, a lesson to knock the impudence right out of his eyes for ever, and keep him down in his gutter.

'Thon's a pretty little tune that you were playing,' said Brian Burns. 'Would you care to tell us the name of it?' The rhetorical question was offered with a horrible gentleness. I knew that whatever Colm said, it would not affect the out-come. Brian liked to play games with the terror-struck, to make them stammer and squirm in the desperate hope that they might find some way in which they could placate him.

'I was playin' Kevin Barry.' Colm's voice was insulting and shrill as Nanny's on one of her venomous days. The ballad of Kevin Barry, a student hanged by the British for shooting a soldier dead in Dublin in 1920, is of all songs guaranteed to rouse cold rage in the Loyalist breast, and hearing him, all fear left me. I could have cheered and applauded; instead, I reached out my right hand and picked up my heavy school-bag by the loops of its leather backstraps. Colm had not played Kevin Barry. He had been playing a jig of the most inoffensive possible kind, and every one of us knew it – which made worse the fact, already plain for anybody to see, that this half-starved little runt of a Taig was using the song as an insult, to show he was up and fighting, and not fruitlessly seeking to please his attackers by meekness or flattery.

For a frozen second, the three stood scandalised, gaping at him; and then the Heavies seized him, each taking an arm and twisting it up behind his shoulder blades so the mouth-organ slithered out of his hands and fell amidst the litter. Brian Burns, with a composure that was very chilling to see, slapped his face methodically – left, right, left, so his whole body jerked like a puppet, and then bent and picked up the harmonica, holding it above his head with an air of admonition that would one day become familiar among his congregation. 'And this filthy auld thing,' he said, 'is fit for nothing but the canal.' Stretching up, he bent backwards a little, preparing to lob it above our heads. It was now or never for me, and my fury was like a delirium. The straps gave a very wide swing to my full and knobbly schoolbag, and by luck I caught Brian's chest just where ribcage gives way to stomach, and winded him completely. He went down as though I had shot him, but I hardly saw where he fell. Surprise was my only ally and the whirl of the schoolbag a battle song. I took the nearest Heavy a little lower down, and was pleased but no longer astonished to see him stagger and crumple, clutching at the crotch of his trousers. As I swung drunkenly away, now propelled by the weight of the satchel, Dick Bond, the sole target left and hampered by holding Colm, seemed a laughably easy assignment: and indeed, shockingly, I *was* laughing, I remember that quite well – standing poised to strike Dick and listening to the sound of my own laughter that seemed to be coming from somewhere else, and was suddenly swept away by the noise of the bus trundling over the bridge and into the Mall beside us.

The conductor stuck his head out of the door. Instantly my

schoolbag fell, and hung innocently beside me. Colm wriggled from Dick's grasp (a limp hold that now was unworthy of being described as a Heavy's) and as one behind the other, we picked our way between gasping Brian and writhing Joe, Colm picked up his harmonica and stuck it back in his pocket.

'What's been going on out there?' the conductor enquired good-humouredly. 'All the boys fighting over you, Ginger?' and he gave my carroty hair a tweak. He knew those big lads quite well, the ones fooling round all over the grass; he often saw them together, all grammar-school kids, and the best of friends. He reached up and jangled his bell, and Colm and I with one accord sat down beside each other, a move we would never have thought to make on an ordinary day, but which seemed to follow naturally from what had gone before it. Yet we were uneasy together. It was as if the shell of innocence and make-believe that had protected our childhood had suddenly been shattered, exposing us to the glare of adult emotions and adult facts, and arousing a new awareness. A self-consciousness we had never before experienced was there, despite the shared victory and the shared seat, and both of us were embarrassed.

At length Colm broke the silence. Without looking at me he said, 'How did ye know where to hit them?'

I glanced at him miserably. I knew nothing of anatomy, and my initial success with my schoolbag had been as surprising to me as the blow to the solar plexus must have been to the unwary Brian. As for Joe, it was true I had heard that you must not hit people below the belt, but I had not aimed deliberately; the arc of the schoolbag had simply dropped, and when it had clobbered Joe . . . I felt suddenly sick and frightened. Supposing I had injured them? And the pain I had inflicted: a little while ago I had felt exhilaration at the sight of it. Now I felt nausea.

'I didn't,' I said wildly. 'I tell you I didn't know. I just wanted to stop them beating you up. I can't fight. I know nothing of fighting.'

Colm turned towards me slowly. 'Ye fought like Finn MacCoul. All Ireland couldn't have matched you – and you with only a schoolbag.' His eyes were bold and appraising. 'And all the size of you! You're a great wee lassie, Alison.'

This was not a Colm I recognised. He had never looked at me like that, and though the voice was his own, his manner and his bearing were of someone very much older, someone offering a tribute with the serious courtesy that a man might show to a woman. And the woman in me responded, beneath the fierce blush and the gym-slip and the tangle of flaming hair, with a surge of dizzying pleasure and pride that transformed the bus into a carriage and restored all the warmth to the spoilt afternoon.

Yet, looking back, I see that the crack that let in the new knowledge was already beyond mending. The violence and fear of that summer day had woken us from a dream that had been the protective fabric of the childhood we shared together. Even if we had been given the time, we could not have found a way to sustain the old relationship, for its essence was unworldliness: we had taken a bite from the apple, and the world was there to stay.

There are two hospitals in Killycreel. The larger, the County General, built around what was once the old workhouse, expands from year to year, and is like a small concrete town in itself, made up of unfinished buildings, prefabricated structures, Nissen huts and mobile homes, all designed to be speedily removed when the long-planned modern extension is finally completed. No one knows when this will be, but construction work proceeds noisily and dustily and slowly, a perennial harassment to patients and staff. The County copes admirably with these difficult conditions, but the personal

47

touch is missing; it has grown too big and too busy for that. By contrast, on Moygarriff Hill, the Old Killycreel Infirmary provides a friendly atmosphere and a minimum of facilities. Ambulances trail to and fro taking 'Moy' patients down to the County for X-rays or specialised treatments, but the passengers say they are glad to get back: the Moy is a home from home, and although there's a chance you might meet your end there from the want of advanced equipment, at least it would not be a faceless death. The County could swallow you whole in its maze of makeshift corridors where nobody bids you good morning, and where visiting hours are so short and strict that you barely can see your kin, and your name has got to be strapped to your wrist because otherwise no one remembers who you are or where you came from. Yes, the Moy is the place to be, no matter if it is old-fashioned, at least you don't lose your identity there.

My father was in the Infirmary now, being treated like a king in the yellow brick building endowed and built by Killycreel's wealthy burghers when his grandfather was Mayor of the town at the end of the century. A portrait of my great-grandfather (who chaired the first Board of Governors and was one of the principal founders) still hangs in the entrance hall, and any McMurtry is welcome as a very special patient. I was greeted with great extravagance when I mentioned my father's name, and the elderly nurse who showed me his room took my hand and pressed it in condolence. 'Such a lovely man! And your poor Mammy too! It's just a sin and a shame. They're not human, the ones that does them things.' She paused outside the door. 'It's shot they should be, not imprisoned.' Her face lost its kindly expression. It became avid and implacable, the face behind the gun, a gun held and fired in morality's name, and instinctively I drew back from her, alarmed by the sudden appearance of a look pitiless and cold as the terrorism we both deplored.

'Here's your daughter now, Mr McMurtry.' She stood back from the doorway and motioned me in.

My father was propped up in bed, with a dressing over one temple and a black eye showing beneath it. He looked so completely unlike himself on the high anonymous bed with its metal frame and pulley and its sky-blue cotton cover, that I actually paused on the threshold saying 'Daddy?' foolishly, like a child puzzled by some unlooked-for disguise.

My father is usually of exceptionally solid appearance. Florid-cheeked and soberly dressed, his respectable suits are like bark on a tree, as much a part of his person as his spectacles seem to be part of his face. But tonight the high colour was gone, together with the glasses and the reassuring suiting. Seen against the stark white of the pillows and sheets, with the bandage askew on his head, he looked poignantly defenceless and at the same time much younger; and when our greetings were over, to avoid showing my distress, I tried to make a joke of it, 'You don't look a day older than Jimmy – a bit of excitement must suit you!'

He laughed. 'Don't say that to Jim. He's already told your mother that I'm in my second childhood!'

The smile left his face rather too swiftly, and I added hastily, 'But your poor head, how's that? Is it giving you pain?'

'Not a whit!' He spoke with decision. 'Sure, my head's made of wood, that's well known in these parts.' He tapped it gingerly. 'There you are, same old sound! Nothing wrong with it now, except it turns a bit giddy when I'm walking about.' He caught hold of the hoist and heaved himself up, grimacing. 'It's the old ribs that's the bother, and they won't take long to mend. There's no more can be done for me here anyway, so I'm twisting their arms a little, and I reckon I'll get them to sign me out sometime over the weekend. I've a lot of work needs attending to . . .'

'Now look here, Daddy,' I said, 'let's not start any nonsense about running straight back to the office. The yards can take care of themselves for a while. You need a bit of rest. I'm sure Jimmy can carry on for you.'

My father frowned. 'That's as may be. He's a bold lad, our Jim.' He avoided my eye, and plucked irritably at the covers. 'But I'm not sure it's boldness that's needed. Look what happened the other day! Have you spoken of it to your mother?'

'Only briefly,' I said. 'I was late. Besides, Brian Burns called to see her.'

My father shook his head. 'He's been round here too – a great friend of Jim's, or so he likes to tell me. Why, the man should be in the asylum! He stood here raving away about Pits of Hell and the Whore of Rome, and Nurse Magee standing beside him with "Catholic" written all over her face, as he very well could see. I got rid of him fast, but I didn't expect he'd be straight up the hill to see Noreen. God help your poor mother, she's moidered enough. All she wants is to see me go – retire from the business and leave it to Jim. Well, I'll be sixty-five in a year or two, and enough's enough. McMurtry's yards have gone from father to son for more than a hundred and fifty years – I'd be proud to see Jimmy run them.' He bent closer to me, his voice suddenly sharp. 'But I'm telling you, Alison, he'll have to watch his step a bit, he'll need prudence as well as enthusiasm. We've enough orders in for a twelve-month – why go out and arrange to supply a company known to be working for the army and the police force? There's not a Nationalist in the place who won't see a political stand in a contract with Rice and Irvine; Billy Rice has been known for years as a Protestant hardliner, and now he's a D.U.P. Councillor ...' There were footsteps in the corridor, and he stiffened. 'Well, we shall see. If that's Jimmy now, you can judge for yourself, for the matter has got to be settled.'

He looked suddenly very weary and I stood up as Jim came in, in a half-unconscious endeavour to put myself between them, an impulse so clearly ridiculous that I hastily stepped up to him and gave him a kiss of welcome. Jim and I are like oil and water these days, and yet when I first see him there is always a moment when I can make these gestures without hypocrisy: I was once as thrilled to see Jimmy as I was to see Killycreel, and the old emotion still lasts long enough for me to keep up appearances. Although Jimmy finds this more difficult, he patted me heartily on either shoulder and managed a smile, 'Hello, stranger! I'm glad to see you can still find the time to visit us!' (I visit Killycreel at least twice a year, and more frequently if my parents do not come to London; but as if I had not enough vices, Jim includes inconstancy as one of my principal failings.) I ignored this from long experience and his point made, Jim left the subject alone. We chatted quite pleasantly about Heather and the children; and about my own son, Robin; and of how soon Father might hope to get home; and I explained again that I'd brought the car, rather than come by air, so that I could do some business with a client in County Antrim who had some pictures for me to value and bring back to London (an expense-account trip, remarked Jimmy), and I answered, without sounding heated, that it meant I could stay for four days instead of the weekend only, and wasn't that very fortunate? December was one of our busiest times . . .

'Well, we're busy here too,' Jim said, 'and I must have a word or two with Pop, if you'll excuse us, Alison.' He picked up his briefcase and opened it. 'I've dealt with most of the mail – there's a couple of letters among this lot that had better have your signature.' Still talking, he passed up some papers. 'The *Fair Kathleen* came in on the evening tide just before I left, she'll start unloading tomorrow. The assessors came down – very decent they were. There shouldn't be any delay on the claim for criminal damages. They've wrote off three lorries entirely, and I've ordered some replacements; we

51

must get the stock away and not leave it building up in the yards – we may not be so lucky the next time.'

My father had wedged his spectacles lopsidedly back on his nose, with one earpiece stretched round the bandage. Apparently deaf to Jim, he was thumbing through the papers, his lips soundlessly mouthing sentences, one finger tracing the progress of his eyes from line to line. He looked a sick man, hardly fit for the task, but in fact he always reads slowly. He does not approve of the habit of scanning a page with your eyes, which he thinks is too perfunctory when dealing with correspondence. Now he signed two letters and folded them up, and extracted a third with care from the pile of documents still in his hands.

'This timber contract,' he said, 'maybe I didn't make myself clear to you? I don't propose to sign it. In the first place, we couldn't fulfil it in time, not without putting it ahead of orders from regular customers that have been on our books much longer. We owe no debt to Rice and Irvine, and I'll not have them jumping the queue with this kind of ignorant demand. That's how you lose good clients.'

He paused and looked straight at Jimmy. 'In the second place,' he said, 'this is a political contract, and I want no part nor parcel of it. We don't need it. There's no point in taking it. Not here in Killycreel. Rice and Irvine may build for the army, but they're not sitting on the border. We can't handle this sort of business. Not in these difficult days.'

Jim's face remained impassive. 'Rice and Irvine needs its wood, Pop. Someone of us has to see to it.'

Father frowned. 'Well, it's not our job. There's a lot of bad boys round Killycreel, and well you know it, Jimmy. We've got to steer clear of contracts that will bring trouble on our heads.'

There was a silence, and Jim got up and walked across to the window. 'Look you, Pop,' he said, 'this contract is not a matter of choice. Billy Rice is a Loyalist Councillor, and his firm's in need of timber. It's suggested that this consignment should be supplied by us.'

He stopped, and my father said blankly, 'Just what do you mean, "suggested"?'

'I mean we've been asked to supply it. When you're asked you don't say no.' His voice rose angrily. 'All right, then! We've been ordered to supply it!'

He turned round and faced his father, gripping on to the end of the bed. 'How the hell do you think we survive here then, with the Old Town crawling with Provos, and three roads across the border without any proper patrols, and our sort outnumbered four to one? Do you think we would last five minutes if they didn't see we're protected?' His harsh voice suddenly fell. 'Well, there's a price for protection, and just now it's this timber contract. We've got to keep in with our own kind or else we'll get blown to hell. Look at what's already happened! You've no choice, and you shouldn't want one. We're not going to save the Province by letting down our friends. You're an Ulsterman like I am,' he leant forward, his knuckles whitening, 'and I'm warning you now! If you turn this down, it won't take you long to find that no Loyalist likes a traitor.'

'That's blackmail!' my father said furiously. 'I'll sign no contract at pistol point! You can tell that to your friends.'

For a moment they glared at each other, like enemies poised for battle. Then my father said more gently, 'You don't know what you're saying, son. McMurtry's has never needed to give favours for protection. And we don't need to now – so long as we don't go signing this sort of thing. We've a reputation for decency . . .'

'Are you daft?' Jimmy shook the bed-rail. 'There's a war on in this Province! And what you talk of as decency is turning your back on your own. That's not decency, that's cowardice – blethering of bloody tolerance while the Brits and the Irish between them sell you down the path to Rome!'

He flung out his hand contemptuously. 'Look at you – why are you lying here? Because you put some old Fenian on the security gates, and he goes and lets in his Provo son, and a colleague or two for good measure! It's just luck for you that the boy is too thick to do a proper job: lucky for us too – we're all at risk, thanks to your ideas of decency!'

I saw that my father had gone very pale. 'Did Pat tell them that?' he said, 'or have they lifted Colm?'

Jim snorted. 'They've lifted no one. You've got to be caught with the bomb in your hands in front of the whole bloody town, before you get lifted nowadays. But we all know Colm Hourican, and the crowd he goes around with – they've been in the IRA since the day they left St Christopher's. Jesus, if we had the Specials . . .'

We waited until it was over. It was all quite familiar to me. In Killycreel the B-Specials were recalled with particular gusto. Their local knowledge had been so great that they could make arrests without the inconvenience of uncovering proof or evidence; they had realised that a bomb in your car or a bullet through your head would be all the reward a man could expect if he went looking for it. They simply *knew* who was guilty. They could pick out the real bad lads from the wide boys and the wastrels. They could smell a Fenian coming. They had wasted no time on witnesses who were frightened to testify. They had just gone in (here Loyalist tones grew loud and hoarse with emotion) and lifted the dirty bastards without fuss or delay, or any bloody nonsense about corroboration. But the Bs were gone, more's the pity: the whole of the RUC and the weight of the British Army was no substitute for the Specials. Grand men. Not a Catholic in Ulster but had heeded the power of the Bs.

When the diatribe had finished, my father enquired, 'And how's Patsy?' as if it had never been spoken.

Jimmy's face flushed a sullen red at this determination to

ignore the point he was making. 'I don't know how he is, for I haven't enquired; but I'll tell you one thing,' he said, 'he's not coming back to McMurtry's. The thing's outrageous entirely. A Provo on the security gates! The boys are fit to be tied; there'll be violence done if he shows his face. If it had been up to me, I'd have had him out of there years ago.'

'But it wasn't,' my father said. 'And what's more, it isn't up to you now – you overreach yourself, Jimmy. I've employed Wee Patsy Hourican for forty years and more. We were down in the yards together before you were ever thought of, and I've never had call to fault him; no, not in the past, nor today.

'Away home!' he continued coldly, and he picked up the timber contract and drew a neat line through it. 'I've let you have your say. And I haven't liked your manner, or your opinions either – any more than I like the company you choose to keep these days. No, no, that'll do . . .' he waved his hand against Jimmy's interruption. 'I've heard you out, and I'll hear no more. That never was the way that a son should speak to his father, and the least said about it the better.' He did not look up, but added with quelling finality, 'So that will be all for this evening. You run away home to Heather. And if you pass Nurse on your way down the stairs, would you ask her to bring up some tea?'

He did not speak again until Jimmy had gone and the sound of his footsteps had faded. Then he said, 'I'm sorry, Alison. It's not a pretty thing to see a house divided. You deserved a better welcome.'

My father's face does not lend itself to the role of tragedy at the best of times, but this evening with his black eye and crooked spectacles and the rakishly angled bandage, the sorrow in his eyes looked particularly incongruous, and I felt a great tenderness for him, and a pity so sharp that I wanted to cry. I took his hand in mine, uncertain how best to comfort him. In the end I tried tentatively to make as light of the affair as I could. 'It's sure to blow over,' I said. 'You know, Jim, half of what he says is hot air. He's embarrassed about this contract. He has promised and now can't deliver, and he hates to look a fool. I expect he knows Billy Rice personally, since they're both active in the Party, and all this about protection is just "help me, and I'll help you". I shouldn't think it's more than that.'

My father smiled at me wryly, 'You don't believe that, do you? It's just what I used to say, but I don't believe it myself any more. Not now. Mind you, Rice and Irvine is not by any means the first to threaten us in this way – but before Jimmy joined the D.U.P. it wasn't a serious matter: there was goodwill enough for both of us then. Though it's not for me to say, I've been well liked in Killycreel, and I've had a fair name with the Catholics for doing the best I could by them. But my day is nearly done, and since Jimmy put up for the Council and took to public speaking, there's been no mistaking how *he*'ll run the firm. That he got no support from me, is of small account; there he is out in front with the Big Man at the rallies, spouting all that evangelist rubbish about the evils of Rome, and walking the streets of the Old Town on the twelfth with his Loyalist banners, and lobbying for the retrial of that hoodlum Nelson McKee, who was fairly convicted of murder and now claims he was the victim of a set-up job by the IRA that none of the judges could see. Well! No doubt we do need protection by now! But . . .' He suddenly sat bolt upright, 'But by God, I'll take my chance on it! If we're wrecked by the IRA, we'll go down as a decent upright firm destroyed by evil and terrorism – not one that went crawling to bully-boys, all eager and willing to pay for protection against its own townspeople. I tell you, I'll not stoop to bribe paramilitary thugs to defend me! And I won't sign my business away to a son who takes orders from gunmen! Not even to please your mother.'

My father is known as a soft-spoken man, and renowned for his gentleness. I had not heard him speak with such passion before. Now, watching him thump the bed as he brought out 'paramilitary thugs', I felt much the same shock and elation as when Colm had thrown 'Kevin Barry' in the face of the Heavy Brigade, long ago, and with equal courage. But my father was off again before I had time to applaud him.

'Now, this bomb at the works,' he said, 'we only know one thing about it – the boyo who put it there was let in by Patsy Hourican, who was half-killed for his trouble. Well, I'll not hear a word against Patsy; whoever it was he let in, it must have been someone he trusted to do no harm to McMurtry's; and God help him, you couldn't blame him for trusting his family – but the only wrong 'un is Colm. Do you remember him, Alison? When you and Jim were children he used to live up on our hill with poor wee Mrs Magennis. I expect she was too old to rear him, for he's been in and out of trouble of some sort ever since she died; a great shock it must have been to Pat at the time when he first was lifted. But he's never tried to deceive himself. He knew the boy was wild, and he made no excuses for him – that's why the thing doesn't hold water. Patsy knows Colm for the rebel he is, he would never have let him in after dark, and the place deserted. He's caution itself, is Pat: I can't think of one of his own kind who he'd let put a foot through security for any reason whatever, once the works were closed for the night. The only ones he'd have trusted . . .' Here he glanced uneasily at me, 'You'll not be repeating this, Alison? Right? Well . . . would have been somebody who was a personal friend of mine, or a personal friend of Jimmy's: that would have been different entirely. Someone in authority, a respectable, clean-living Protestant.' He laughed without mirth. 'Somebody who felt that a little incident was called for to make me appreciate that no Loyalist likes a traitor?'

He paused and sighed heavily as if all the fight had gone out of him. 'Likely Jimmy is right,' he said, 'I'm an old man and growing soft in the head. But I'd dearly like to see Pat, though they say he remembers nothing at all. I was hoping that you'd take me in to visit him at the County if they let me out on Sunday? If I wait till he's home with his women-folk, I might as well stay in bed for all the chance we'll get to speak. Such a household! Lord knows how he's sane! You'd not credit the number they pack in that room.'

He began to describe to me the conditions I'd find if we went to see Pat in his terraced slum in the Old Town, and I listened as if I had never been there. Even now, half a lifetime away, it would have been hard to mention the visit I had paid to it, without opening up a Pandora's Box of tales within troubling tales, and leaving my father amazed and distressed by how much I had hidden from him at a time when he thought he had known me well. So I sat there silently, thinking of another occasion when I had come home from England at almost exactly the same time of year, after a first term at school so distorted by homesickness that it had passed by like a nightmare.

Today's Anglo-Irish children, travelling to their English boarding schools, come and go through Belfast Airport. When the holidays end or begin, the arrivals hall fills with their parents who converge from all the Province and greet each other ecstatically. To the Northern Irishman they present an outlandish appearance, and are largely presumed to be English, a fact which would greatly annoy them if they ever took it in, for they pride themselves on an exclusive and transcendent sort of Irishness that they think is apparent to everyone, and not only guarantees a pronounced superiority over those brought up like my father (who speak with local accents and educate their young either in their immediate

58

neighbourhoods or at fee-paying schools in the Province) but also over all Englishmen. Perhaps dying ascendancies are prone to this sort of illusion when their numbers are down to a handful in the countries they have colonised, but when I left Killycreel I had never met such people and their arrogance astounded me.

Unfortunately, however, in 1963 it had not yet become normal practice to fly children to their boarding schools. Everyone was still in the habit of travelling by sea, which took a whole agonising night, and increased the feeling of severance so acutely, and magnified the miles to such an appalling degree, that you could not have felt much farther from home if you had sailed the Atlantic. That melancholy Irish description of journeying to England – to be 'going across the Water', never sounded so dreary as when your ferry drew out from the quay at nine o'clock in the evening and steamed down the lough through the shipyards and oil refineries, past the lights that you knew must be Holywood, Cultra and Newtownabbey, Helen's Bay and Carrickfergus, till you reached the open sea and the glimmer that was Bangor gave way to a heaving darkness that swallowed up everything you loved. Even now, I cannot stand on the deck of the Liverpool ferry as it leaves the Irish coastline without echoes of that desolation coming painfully back to me with the sharp salt wind that tells you that you have cleared the headlands, or hear the routine announcement about visitors going ashore without feeling a trace of the panic that the words brought to me in my school days, when they seemed like the very knell of doom.

My school was in Lincolnshire, a county of fen and farmland that struck me as deeply depressing. Monotonous as the ocean, its huge fields stretched away without a relieving contour in any direction whatever. I had never seen such flatness, and it seemed a dismal thing and almost evilly ugly to eyes accustomed to hillsides. When I came to read *Childe Roland*, I am afraid to say that I always pictured the journey taking place through the wastes of Lincolnshire – 'Grey plain all round: nothing but plain to the horizon's bound. I might go on; nought else remained to do,' was a perfect description of arriving at Swalethorpe where presently, when I too 'shut my eyes and turned them on my heart', I was to find my certainties dissolving in bitterness and confusion. But that was later; my first term at Swalethorpe was a black-and-white affair and left no room for comparison or reflection. Home was a paradise, lost and desired – school was unendurable: and if sometimes I looked up from the depths of my wretchedness and caught a glimpse of the sky, I buried myself again quickly, too traumatised by homesickness to wish to comprehend it. Instead, like a person who has lost a limb, I dwelled obsessively on what had been a part of me. My home and my family. Colm. Dunvarden Moor and the mountains. The voices, faces, places that made up the world I knew – all these I missed individually with a sharp and frightening anguish, and collectively with a sick lassitude that lay like a knot in my chest and took away my appetite and my very will for survival. Perhaps prisoners pass through this awful malaise, for woven among all the strands of yearning, I missed my freedom most acutely. I was accustomed to living without interference. I had made my own way to school, had ridden my bike and caught the bus and shopped by myself in the New Town, or wandered all over the moors alone. For me, this liberty was a vital part of my self-respect, and the loss of it added horribly to my feelings of bereavement. As time passed, even I could see that my education at Swalethorpe was the gate to a much greater freedom, the freedom to think independently, but at first nothing mattered to me except the Christmas holidays and getting back to Dunvarden. At the start of the term, this prospect seemed so faint and far away that I had hardly dared to consider it, but suddenly it was upon me, creeping up almost undetected in the fog of my distress and breaking through it victoriously, transforming my surroundings. Now that Killycreel was within my reach I regained my identity, and with it the spirit to explore my hated penal settlement and find it was not quite as bad as I thought. There even appeared to be one or two congenial people about, despite the fact they were English, and one had to admit that the jailors were kind . . . Exhausted with misery, and almost hysterical with relief, I joined the Ulster contingent for the train journey back to Liverpool. The others were strangers to me: Swalethorpe had been picked by my mother because she had chanced to discover that two other Irish families were sending their daughters there and, although she did not know them, she knew *of* them, which was better – no child from her own social circle would make so distinguished a friend, or prove such a valuable starting point for my future in high society. In fact, I did form a vague friendship with the only one of the three who was of approximately my own age, but this was based on our exile more than real compatibility; as we crossed the Irish Sea we would lie on our bunks with our faces turned to the pitching walls of our cabin and weep in companionable regret for what briefly seemed to be the same loss and the same Northern Ireland – but fundamentally we both knew that this was not the case. Sally lived in a castle near Omagh, where her stalwart family attempted to go on existing as they had in the last century, defying both isolation and threat by breeding extensively and opening the house in summer to a small and indifferent public. This was very far from my background, and though Sally did ask me to stay for her brother's twenty-first birthday dance, the experience was unnerving. The elite of the Province was gathered there, and a great many English guests, and the sound of their public-school voices made me very glad that Jimmy had spurned the throw away offer 'do bring your brother too', for the pleasures of the regatta at home and the Yacht Club hop that followed it.

True friendship can rise above this sort of thing, but Sally was not a true friend, and I felt I had nothing to offer her – not even the whiff of novelty that Dunvarden might hold for an English girl. The very Irishness that bound us loosely together at school, at home became an impediment to knowing each other better, and real contact stayed confined to the intimate nights that we shared on the boat. The other two girls from Swalethorpe were sisters and slept together. They were older than we were by far, and usually managed to make a rendezvous with a crowd of noisy acquaintances whom we admired from a distance. But on that first holiday I was too overwrought and excited to pay them the slightest attention. I did not go down to the cabin until long after we had sailed, and was up at four in the morning to make sure I would not miss our landfall, although our scheduled arrival was still three hours away.

In those days, on a first-class ticket, the overnight crossing was dignified. Stewards showed you your cabin and carried your bags and woke you with cups of tea. You could even have a bath if you wished – salt or fresh – and the water was scalding. The restaurant was discreet and quiet as a dull sea-side hotel, and the bar was an astonishing place with panelled walls and a structure that looked like a minstrels' gallery built of wood at the farther end. But at four o'clock in the morning the atmosphere was desolate. The restaurant was shuttered. The lounge was hushed and dim, with the few unfortunate passengers who had failed to find berths sprawled about it in ungainly attitudes of sleep. No one manned the reception desk, and the reassuring attendants in their neat white coats had vanished. The companionways and corridors were deserted, as lifeless and bare as if the ship were abandoned. The engines alone vibrated, alive in the eerie stillness as the ferry laboured ahead, full-steam through the night, and despite the dark and the cold and the frightening silence, I took courage from this and went out on deck. I stood by the bow rail in the wind and the spray of our passage, and watched the wave break silver on the prow of the ship and scud backwards until it melted away, engulfed in the oily black of the sea. I stayed there, half-mesmerised by the water and the throb of the ship and my own fatigue and longing, until I could see the lights of the coast and the channel buoys ahead, and then I turned and went below, like a seaman whose watch had ended. I was home. I was myself again. Even if the vessel went down I could now swim across to the shores of the lough . . . The loneliness of my exile had become as impossible to recall as bygone physical pain, and Swalethorpe itself was unreal as a dream. I was suddenly very hungry. I ordered fruit juice and porridge, two sausages, bacon, eggs, tomatoes, toast, everything I could see. When Sally sat down beside me, I started, for I had forgotten her. She belonged to the Other Side, and I was already at Killy-creel and out on the moor with Colm. Perhaps we would have frost this winter, and there would be ice on Lough Rhinn, which was shallow as a puddle, and we could go up and skate there, Jim's old boots would do Colm nicely . . . I finished the bacon and eggs and started on toast and marma-lade like someone refuelling an engine. Food becomes a seri-ous business when you have been pining away and are suddenly called back to life again.

After breakfast I went outside to watch us berth. I did not expect my father to come for an hour or so. It was fifty miles to Dunvarden, and that could seem quite a long way if you started out before six o'clock on a dark December morning. But when the ferry came in alongside, there he was, standing on the quay in his gaberdine raincoat and Homberg hat and a woollen scarf tucked round his collar – his unvarying winter costume. In the years that have passed since then, he has come to meet me scores of times at habours and stations and airports, and yet when I picture him waiting for me, I see him as he was that day, too far away for hailing, with his head tipped back in the lamplight as he scanned the passenger decks for my face. As we drew nearer, I could see his anxiety and his eagerness in the way he kept leaning sideways, bending backwards the better to search the ship's sides, and I found myself suddenly aware of him as a person – not just a father-figure who could neither suffer nor change nor do wrong, but a person exactly like me, who had risen needlessly early too because of his excitement at the thought of recovering what he had lost.

This perception was new to me, and demoralised me completely. My own plight had been trouble enough to survive: it had not occurred to me that my parents might be missing me too, or worse still, might be seriously worried as to whether or not they had done a wise thing in sending me away, and the knowledge that they were unhappy as well was really too much to contend with. They had confidently assured me that they knew it was for the best that I should be schooled in England, and I had never doubted them. Parents knew about such matters, and they could not be wrong. Even at my very worst moments I had trusted their omniscience: if they said that this was the proper course at least no mistake had been made, no alternative was possible, and the outcome would be to my benefit. To suspect the truth of this judgment was to destroy the last shreds of confidence that sustained me. The last thing I wanted to see that morning was a mortal, prone to error and racked with worry about his daughter's welfare. Nor had I bargained to feel the painful and protective love that filled me as I looked down on him – not Daddy-the-Institution, but someone who cared for me in much the same way as I cared about him. It was all too much to handle. Tears poured down my face like a waterfall, and I mopped at them furiously with the hairy edge of my uniform cloak. I was suddenly filled with resentment. They had cast me out. They were not really sure that it was for the best. Their opinion was not infallible. And on top of this disillusionment, they were asking me to love them in a new and exhausting way that somehow involved *my* pitying *them*. Well, I simply would not do it. I would not throw myself in my father's arms as I would have done yesterday. I would not let him see me weeping, for relief or joy or sadness or whatever it was that was making me cry. If they chose to send me away, they had no right to expect me back unchanged by the experience.

I turned from the rail and my father's face, and sullenly made my way below to the cabin to fetch my bags. I knew he had not seen me, and that I had only to call out to him to bring him instant pleasure, but I did not look back or hurry myself. Already I was consciously drawing satisfaction from the thought that I could prolong his uneasiness, the first fruit of the new resentment that would yield so abundantly.

I was always completely unable to talk to my family about Swalethorpe. Even when I had made my peace with it, I did not know how to convey the broader horizons and flexible modes of thought that I had discovered there, nor explain how important they were to me; and on that first holiday I could find no means of expressing the violent emotional turmoil that had torn me to pieces since last we met – I was not accustomed to say that sort of thing to my parents; our contact had always been simple. Like any little animal, I had come back every night to the place where nurture and comfort were given without question, and where love needed no declaration. In our house a 'How are you?' referred to your physical well-being and not to your sensitivities (which, unlike tonsillitis or toothache or bouts of 'flu, did not thrust themselves forward for comment), but as long as we were together in the natural family context of a life lived day by day, observation and instinct had kept us in touch. Once I went away to school, the bond was broken, the link was gone: I had no idea how to cross the extraordinary chasm between us –

'How are you, darling?'

'Oh, very well, thank you.'

'And how about school? You don't give much away in your letters.'

'School's all right . . .' I avoided their eyes and scraped noisily at my empty plate.

'Good gracious, look at the child! She'll be eating the dishes before she's done! Would you like some more pudding, Alison?'

'Are they feeding you properly over there?'

'Yes please! Well, the food's not bad – a bit funny, but there's lots of it. Could you pass the sugar, Jimmy?'

'Don't take the whole bowl! Where's your manners?'

'Now Jimmy, let Alison be! Can't you see the poor girl is famished? I expect it was the journey. Did the boat make you sea-sick, lovey?'

'Well, a bit . . .' This was untrue, but a handier way of explaining fatigue, second helpings and four spoons of sugar than declaring I scarcely had eaten a bite since the day I went away on account of the knot in my stomach. Now the term was over and done, I wanted to put it right out of my mind, to pretend it had never happened, to go on as if nothing was different at all. That seemed the only way to re-establish contact and obliterate the feeling of anger and alienation that had swept over me on the boat when I first set eyes on my father.

After lunch I took my bicycle, which seemed smaller than I remembered it, and when I had wiped off the cobwebs, I free-wheeled down the hill to the meadow behind O'Hagan's. This field afforded a view of the road and the bus stop beneath it, and had always been very useful as a look-out post and a meeting place. Up against the Northern hedge, in a fine commanding position, there stood the remains of a calf creep. Two rickety posts nailed together made a prop at either end for the piece of corrugated tin that formed the roof of the shelter and still gave some protection from the rain, though the strong wind from the West had long ago caused the whole structure to list drunkenly to leeward, and to keep dry you had to bend double and crouch at the easterly end.

It was good to be back in the calf creep. For the first time since leaving for England, I felt at ease and happy. I had half an hour to spend before the school buses would start to arrive, but the place made a pleasure of waiting, and I felt delightfully secure. The smell of rust and rain and decaying vegetation soothed me with familiarity. The clouds were thinning above me; small ragged chinks of sky were appearing above the twin mountains, and insipid shafts of yellow betrayed where the sun was setting behind the hills to my right. It was all as I remembered it. I was not even excited at the thought of seeing Colm again, because only yesterday (or so it seemed), I had met him here on what passed for a fine winter's evening – this year, last year, next year maybe – it did not matter at all, he would stay the same for ever, like the watery light over the valley, and the creaking and the tapping of the corrugated tin where the nails lifted out of the rotting wood ... So I sat there thankfully, at home in the sour pasture, peering out through last summer's thistles, and waited in great contentment for my friend to be brought back to me.

There were half-a-dozen buses in the regular after-school

convoy. The first bus was always commandeered by St Malachy's High School (which was just behind the terminus, and thus unfairly advantaged), and when that was full, the remnants of its pupils overflowed into the second vehicle, which then remained half-empty until the St Christopher's children arrived from the other end of the town to take the unoccupied places. By that time, the next three in line had fallen to the two Protestant schools, so the surplus from St Christopher's was forced to squeeze into the last bus of all. This bus always fell behind, for it had to pick up the stragglers – but Colm was seldom upon it. Sharp elbows and strong homing instincts made him pretty sure to find a place on the coveted second bus, and that day I was rather surprised when it did not stop at O'Hagan's. (Bother Colm, he might have hurried ... but, of course, he was not expecting me.) A pause, then the next three came, in a bunch, one behind the other. It made me feel very strange to see Dorothy Kinney, in gold and maroon, step down and wave to the driver, just as I had done a thousand times. In fact now the light was dim, I had the uncanny feeling that it was myself I was watching, and I was relieved when her father clanked up in his old van and drove her away from the bus stop, for the sight of her filled me with rancour.

The calf creep had lost its attraction; I crawled out and perched on the gate and glared angrily down the deserted road. It was very unpleasing to find I was jealous of Dorothy Kinney, and the bitterness was back again ... Damn this bus, what had happened to it? But at last I heard it come, changing gear on the hill, and then there it was, with the lights turned on inside it so that you could see the children in their gaudy St Christopher's blue, packed as tightly as sheep at the market. Yet I knew there was something the matter: the speed, the sound of the engine; it was going much too fast, it was not going to stop at O'Hagan's, it was not going to stop for Colm ... I stood up on the gate and shouted and waved my arms in the air as if I was slowing a runaway horse – until I fell into the brambles, and there I sat for a long time, too disappointed to cry or even to pull out the prickles.

At length I began to rally. There were countless explanations: maybe Colm had been kept in; perhaps he was sick, or had just stayed in town; it was pointless to feel dejected, and foolish to wait any longer since the next bus was not due for another hour. The best thing to do was to go and visit Nanny; she would know what had happened to Colm.

I puffed back up the hill, with panic grumbling like hunger in some uncontrollable part of me, and turned off the road and on to the track beside the dolmen stone without looking where I was going, and fell heavily off my bicycle. Then I saw that the ruts were narrower, for the mound in the centre had grown, and the shaggy banks had converged on each side so they caught on the spokes and the pedals. For a moment I was bewildered. It was true that Magennises' Lane was habitually neglected, but I never had seen it impassable; after all, there were the bicycles, and Pat with the car for Mass, and the van from the mobile grocery ... I stood thoughtfully, rubbing my bruises, and stared with increasing uneasiness at the lumpy tussocks of grass, growing unbroken in the wheel tracks. No car had been this way for several months; I was sure of it.

I went forward cautiously until I could see the cottage, but there was no glow from the windows although it was past lighting-up time. Outside I could see my way despite the dusk, but inside I knew it would be blind dark: where was Nanny? My deepening apprehension was becoming a certainty. I wrenched the lamp off my handlebars and ran across the enclosure where Nanny kept her livestock, but no dog barked at me, and no hissing came from the filthy hutch where the two geese should have been roosting. Yet I could not, would not, believe it. I hammered on the half-door in a frenzy of incredulity, and shouted wildly for Colm, for Nanny, for Paschal even, until my fists were sore and my throat was aching with tears and fright, and my voice began to fail me; then I hurled myself against the wood. The bottom remained fast, but the top of the door burst open, and made bold by desperation, I heaved myself over the threshold and dropped down on the earthen floor.

Nobody had cleared out the cottage, that was almost the worst thing about it. Left empty, it would have been totally changed, and might not have smelled so bad – but there had been little of value to take, I could see that by looking round me, though I never had thought about it before. Nanny's personality, and the warmth of the fire and the glow of the lamp and the steam from the boiling potatoes had somehow obscured the poverty. The room had never looked bare, and even the dirt had been living, renewed and augmented daily by the dross of four people's existence. Now decay was in the air, so thick you could almost touch it. There was mildew on the table, the stuffing was falling out of the couch, the cooking-pot still hung above the cold fire where the autumn rain, running down the inside of the chimney, had turned the soot into a sticky mess that oozed out on to the hearth and glinted in the light of my lamp. Damp was already blackening the paper; toadstools sprouted upon the woodstack, and, most horrible of all, two bundles of feathers lay prone on the floor just underneath the window, one brown and one white, the sad remains of two of Nanny's hens, no doubt overlooked and shut in by mistake. The hens had used the house freely, and occasionally roosted in a row on the foot of Nanny's bed.

Nanny's bed – the thought was appalling. The back room had always spelled sorcery, with its acrid smell of bodies and its aura of guilt and pain, sick people and dead babies, and though I had found that intriguing in the days when the world was a sunnier place, the prospect of facing it now in this context of devastation was too ghastly to be considered. Shock had held me as still as a statue, but now I turned and fled as if the Devil was on my heels.

I pounded back to Dunvarden and burst into the kitchen where my mother was at the stove.

'What's happened to Nanny Magennis?'

'My goodness child, don't shout! Poor little Mrs Magennis was gathered back in September. It must have been just after you went away to school – she'd had a bad heart for a long time, you know. In the end she went very quickly.'

My legs were wobbling strangely and I leaned against the door. I had known she would tell me that Nanny was dead, the cottage had shown me that plainly. Nonetheless, hearing it was terrible. I stood there in a daze, and watched her back as she basted and stirred, turning the roasting potatoes.

'At least we can pull down that awful old place and get things cleared up,' she said. 'What on earth can people have thought of us, leaving that poor woman there without sanitation or anything? But the Lord knows, we did our best, and she might have been the Cloughmore stone for all that we could shift her, though we offered both help and money. Well, she's gone now, God rest her soul, and that son of hers hasn't been seen since she died. It seems he took all the savings and there wasn't a mite for the funeral.' She turned round from the stove. 'Why Alison dear, come in by the fire! You look absolutely frozen, you shouldn't have stayed out so long in the cold.'

I went in obediently, and lowered myself into the basket chair before I could trust myself further. Then I said, 'But where is Colm?'

'The boy? Pat Hourican's son? Well, you know what a

decent wee fellow Pat is – he took the child home directly, though apparently he's as wild as they come, and they're all at their wits' end to know what to do about him, or so Pat was telling Daddy. But I daresay he'll settle down in the end. And Paschal – he's been taken in on one of the mental wards at the Moy . . . Would you lay the table, darling? Tea's ready, and we'd better have it as soon as Daddy comes in.'

'I just wondered if I could see Colm?'

It was a terrible visit. Unfitting. Humiliating. I had known from the very start that I should never have made it. Pat had answered the door in his shirt sleeves, looking startlingly naked without his cap, and stared at me vacantly as if he had never seen me before. Then he burst out hurriedly, 'Dear God! If it's not Miss Alison! Is the Daddy looking for me?'

His surprise alone was embarrassing. Besides no one in Killycreel had ever called me Miss Alison, and I didn't like the sound of it.

'No, he isn't,' I said. 'I just wondered . . .' Pat was looking up the road, as if in quest of my father's car, '. . . I just wondered if I could see Colm?'

His expression of astonishment had barely time to change into one of real shock, before his wife emerged from the hubbub behind him. Theresa looked very like Nanny. Her face was hard and thin, and her small black eyes were alert and cold and flickered when she was suspicious, giving her the implacable air of a snake. They were flickering at me then, taking in my lack of confidence and according it no compassion. Although she disliked all Protestants, and particularly decried the privileged and the well-to-do, she expected them to display a code of social behaviour in keeping with their position that at least would be worthy of grudging respect. I had simply no business to be appealing for understanding or help from the likes of the Hourican family, and my presence

72

on her doorstep made her doubly distrustful of me, yet I could not be left standing out on the street, a slur on her hospitality in the eyes of curious neighbours.

'Will ye stand back, Pat?' she said, 'and let the wee lassie in out of the rain before we're all of us foundered?'

It was like stepping into an oven. I was soaked through to the skin from the bicycle ride to O'Hagan's, and the walk up the hill to the Old Town. I could feel myself literally starting to steam as I stood with my back to the door, confronting a living-room crammed wall-to-wall with Pat's extended family. Prams were parked on either side of me, toddlers crawled all over the floor, two babies lay asleep on the couch, and above them a host of faces turned towards me in mute enquiry. A shawled figure by the fire broke the silence in the cantankerous screech of one cut off by deafness. 'Is the wee girl lost then, Patsy? Who is it she's looking for?'

'It's Mr McMurtry's child, Mammy,' said Pat, but the old woman did not hear him, or the note of warning reproof in his voice. She leant forward and bawled at me, 'What is it you're wanting then, daughter dear?' and I yelled back gratefully, before I had time to consider my words, 'It's Colm I wanted to see.'

My reply rang round the cluttered room, as scandalous as blasphemy. It was hardly to be credited that a girl from my family, a creature from another world, should be interested in Colm – but if she were (faces hardened), then what a slut there must be underneath the show of gentility! I was sexually very innocent, but there was no mistaking the contempt and hostility in the score of eyes that observed me, and I felt the hot blood rise and flame in my face at the shame of it. I felt hideously wronged and insulted. At least Nanny had never misjudged me so. But Nanny had gone and died, and left me without protection . . .

Suddenly, I could bear it no longer. Ever since I had

rushed from the cottage, leaving half my childhood behind with two rotting hens in a lifeless room, grief and anger had built up inside until they were like an abcess. Now this final attack on my pride pierced the fragile skin of my self-control by dint of its very unfairness.

'No one told me the cottage was empty!' To my rage, I was starting to cry, but self-pity grew by the instant now all dignity was abandoned, and I shouted and sobbed on wildly, 'No one told me Nanny had died! I saw her every day of my life until they sent me to England, and now I'll never see her again! Why shouldn't I want to find . . .?' I choked to a halt, abruptly aware that the atmosphere had altered, and very much for the better. I had been going to say 'Why shouldn't I want to find Colm?', but my need for immediate comfort was so strong it awoke low cunning, and I ended on a wail of calculated pathos, 'to find out what happened to her?'

There was silence as my outburst faded; but the animus had left it. And then, as though to the room at large, I heard Theresa say, 'Ach, God love her, the poor youngster! She was always up at Mammy's . . .' and I knew that her censure had been withdrawn. I could have tried all my days to find a way to Theresa's heart and never gained an entry, but tears shed for Nanny were passport enough. Mairead was sent to make tea, and I was led in by the fireside, still hiccuping and steaming, and urged to eat cake and sandwiches while everyone treated me to a blow-by-blow tale of the death-bed and a rich account of the funeral. No mention was made of Colm, and I sat there wretchedly, feeling guiltier than I need have done, for my sense of bereavement was genuine, and I had not originally wanted to curry sympathy. But at last, by route of Paschal, we came to Matthew's defection: this was clearly a sore subject, and was glossed over hastily – 'Gone off on his travels! You know Uncle Matt – why, houses wouldn't hold him!'

And as I nodded agreement, Mairead said unhappily, 'Do you think he's fit to mind Colm?'

Theresa frowned at her warningly; and Patsy added quickly (for my benefit, I could see), 'Sure Matthew's fit for anything, there's no better one to handle him. It takes crafty to deal with crafty, and thon child's sheer treachery!'

We returned to the safe ground of Nanny, and the awkwardness was forgotten. Plainly, Colm had been a disaster. Had he run away from home? Had he played truant from St Christopher's? Had the law or the Welfare been after him? All these things and more, most probably. Yet I did not press them again, for in the last hour I had come face to face with the truth half-perceived in the cottage – that the idyll was finally over, that my life had been drastically changed, and that Colm and his friendship were as lost to me as Nanny; and in any sense that mattered, I would never see him again.

Now, sipping another cup of tea as I sat by my father's bedside in a private ward on Moygarriff Hill, I marvelled at the way he could describe Patsy's living-room exactly as I recalled it, yet with such a shift of emphasis that no one could fail to be convinced that its atmosphere was one of guileless feudal devotion. Was I wrong to remember it otherwise? The Theresa now painted for me 'always thought the world of your mother'. *My* last memory of Theresa was of standing outside a closing door and overhearing her say, 'Is there nothing that woman wouldn't do – sending yon poor wee'n over the water? Have ye ever heard the like of it? Sure, Holy Mother o'God, is it stones they have where their hearts should be?' – but I tried to put that from me, and instead to follow my father's voice as he recreated for me the too-hot fire and the too-small room, the smell of crowded bodies, stale fat and babies' bottles; and the faces – more numerous, now that all of the girls were married and a new generation

75

was growing – but essentially the same as before, a close-knit community that represented a dozen homely virtues to my father, since he looked for no collusion and suspected no trickery, and saw Patsy Hourican himself as the very quintessence of fealty. I prayed he was not mistaken.

'We'll go and see Pat,' I said, 'just as soon as you're up and about again and fit to get down to the County. I'll be in again tomorow night, about the same time I should say. I've got to go up to Antrim to do a bit of business: picture hunting in high places. I'm lunching with Lord Glencreagh, but if everything's gone smoothly I should get away soon afterwards.'

'Well, that will please your mother,' he said, and we smiled in complicity, 'Nothing like a lord to cheer her up!' Then he added, his voice growing serious, 'See you tell her all about it, she needs distracting these days. And mind how you go yourself, Alison; we've had enough calamity to do us all for a week or two!'

He lifted a hand in farewell, and I laughed and answered him lightly, half-mimicking my mother, 'And what harm would a person come to at such a good address?'

Drumgarvey House was built towards the end of the eighteenth century, and is large and beautiful and sad, for, although the family ostensibly still lives there, they spend most of the year in London, where the present Lord Glencreagh is a banker. Next morning, as I made my way between the unadorned lawns that ran from the drive to the edge of the ha-ha, and passed the barren conservatory and the windows of the East Wing, blank and white in front of closed shutters, I was struck by the loveless air of institutional management that hung over the house and gardens. Everything was tended neatly, and yet so dispassionately that it seemed to me rather more forlorn than the crumbling but cherished wreckage of Sally's castle in County Tyrone.

My host opened the door in person, somehow conveying to me that pretending to be one's own butler was a most amusing experience. He was an urbane gentleman, with that aura of bonhomie that the Anglo-Irish are wont to assume to show how quaintly Irish they remain, despite all evidence pointing to the contrary. Indeed he was very charming, with a warm hospitality he would not have shown me in his London house, introducing me courteously to his English wife, and his eldest son down from Oxford for the vacation, and a world-weary teenage daughter. His younger son, he said, was still at Eton but naturally would join them later for Christmas. They all loved Christmas in Ireland, brought a crowd of friends over each year and really packed the old house out, nowhere like it for throwing a party . . . Here I stole a glance at the English wife who had seemed sullen and distraught, but the prospect of entertaining her friends did not appear to have cheered her. She advised me to keep on my overcoat. They had only been back three days, and it took some time for the place to dry out, it was always so damp in Ireland, and of course with the house shut up most of the year . . . but then, what could one do? However much you adored it, you could seldom make time to get over. Had I ever been to Ireland before?

'I come from here,' I said. 'My parents live in Killycreel. I'm staying with them at the moment.'

Lord Glencreagh looked at me with new interest. 'Would we know the name?' he said. 'We've got lots of chums in County Down. Could easily have bumped into them.'

His whole manner suddenly grated on me. 'I shouldn't think so,' I said. 'My people are timber importers, and they've never been great socialites.' I knew this was rude, but I rounded it off. 'True Ulster folk, born and bred. My father's name is Carson McMurtry – you will hardly have run across him.'

I met his eye and smiled coldly as I watched him reassess the balance between us. I hoped he would know that I found his Irishness specious, and at the same time I was shamed by my spite. The glaring Englishness of his voice and his appearance made his efforts fail so completely that they should not have made me angry: where he was not personally known, he would instantly be branded as a stranger-from-over-the-water, just as I myself was branded. I wondered if he minded this rejection of his identity, or whether he was blind to it? Perhaps, if you were complacent enough, it was possible to go through all your life believing that because of your seat and your title, the Province would look on you kindly and regard you as one of its own?

Either way, he appeared impervious to my momentary lapse of good manners. With a vague, 'No, I don't think the name rings a bell . . .' he turned towards the door and led me across the stone flags of the hall while he gracefully changed the subject. 'Most of my grandfather's paintings are hanging upstairs,' he said. 'He took the ballroom over and made it into his gallery: he was really quite a collector.' He paused with his foot on the stair, and I saw how loath he was to disperse what was still an intact inheritance. 'Anyway, I hope you like them, most people are rather impressed,' he smiled with disarming frankness, 'and I badly need the money. Lose the house, or sell the pictures, that's the truth of it, I'm afraid. The upkeep's really appalling. The roof leaks. The whole place needs rewiring. Now they've found dry rot in the cellars! And I can't get staff to stay unless I pay them a fortune – it's the troubles . . .' I smiled sympathetically, and made polite non-committal sounds. I had seen nothing on my way through the house to lead me to believe the collection would be exciting, though the paintings around me were pleasant enough.

My forecast was totally wrong, for the ballroom revealed

a treasure-trove of exceptional range and quality – and my host was well aware of it, I could tell by the covert way he watched my reactions as he produced two exquisite Guercino drawings which should have been in a museum – 'I'll hang on to these, by the way. I'm really rather attached to them.' Together they would have raised the money that he needed without looking any farther, but the warning behind the indifferent voice showed plainly in his eyes. In our business we are well trained in tact, and this was not the moment to point out that his vague attachment was costing him in the range of a hundred and fifty thousand pounds. Instead, I was able to say that, viewed in the most basic terms, the luminous van der Neer would solve his dry rot problems, and the landscape by Nasmyth, with its subtle blend of classical style and natural northern beauty would go far to putting the roof to rights. I suggested we divide our selection of pictures between two sales, so that if the first three or four far exceeded their agreed reserves, we could hold back the rest until we had had another chance to talk the matter over; in other words, he could keep them. Our firm always deals this way, and it carries very little risk. Once the wrench of parting is over, few customers want their possessions returned, but at this first delicate stage, when the owner is reluctant, distrustful and protective, diplomacy pays off handsomely. No one likes to be plundered for gain and our reputation for diffidence attracts a lot of customers who resent the need for an auction house and would gladly send us away empty-handed, could they afford it.

This applied to Lord Glencreagh, but the pleasure of showing his paintings to someone who shared his delight made a fragile rapport between us that eased the strain of the morning and, by the time we had finished and the necessary plans had been laid, we both felt almost elated. A perfect auction was pending – a sale of important Old Masters, coming up in April or May and, providing I took the paintings when I went back to London, we could get the photographs rushed through and the details checked again in time to catch the catalogue before it went to the printers. I would fix the travel insurance at once, and contact a local firm of packers to box the pictures on Monday, if I could arrange it. I would meet them here, see the work properly done, and then take the paintings away.

I went down to lunch feeling cheerful. My host, with his English ways and his international paintings, had taken my mind off my family. The gallery at Drumgarvey House could have been light years away from the tensions and troubles of Killycreel, and I had enjoyed the respite and had hoped it would last till the end of the meal. I was therefore dismayed to see that the library had been invaded by several other visitors. Lord Glencreagh led me over to the group by the fire and began by presenting me to a very young man with a worrying squint, 'You've not met Olivia's cousin? Rory Montagu – Alison Lacey. Rory'll know all about Killycreel – he's doing six months on the border.' The young man inclined his head, uncertain what he was expected to say, and Lord Glencreagh passed on breezily, 'Andrew Burleigh-Hall, my agent. I don't know where we'd be without Andrew to look after us. And this is his wife, Sally.'

Sally Burleigh-Hall smiled prettily. She was young and very pregnant. 'You're Charlie's picture expert,' she said. 'Olivia was just telling me that you had come over from London. Don't you think the place is marvellous? We're so happy here, aren't we Andrew? I didn't want to come, but we've been here two years, and honestly we hardly notice the troubles! I was just saying so to Mr Lamont.' She gestured uncertainly to the stocky man beside her, and I met his pale stare with reluctance. I had been cherishing a hope that these guests might not, after all, interfere with the soothing impression that I was far from Ulster, but Mr Lamont soon dispersed it.

'The name's Bill Lamont,' he said, 'of the Forestry Division. Pleased to meet you, Mrs Lacey.' He held out his hand, and I shook it. Unlike the other men, who were casually dressed, he was wearing a suit in honour of the occasion and, even without the accent or the severe dark tie that bore the red hand of Ulster on a white shield at its centre, I would have known him anywhere for a fellow countryman and, despite myself, felt the affinity that kin feels for kin amongst strangers.

Bill Lamont was not correspondingly moved. 'So you're from London, then? I hope you're enjoying your visit?' he said. The question was polite, a native's courtesy to a guest, yet it hardly called for an answer. It was clear from his face and his tone of voice that not only must I be enjoying my stay in his country, but that my escape from London must be like a parole from a prison.

I answered irritably, 'No, I'm not, I'm afraid. Things are bad at home, and I'm worried about my parents,' and added, I felt for the hundredth time, 'I come from Killycreel . . .' but before Bill Lamont could respond to this, a tray of drinks came between us, and as I took my glass of wine and heard him say virtuously, 'No, no, not for me. No, nothing at all. I only drink when I'm thirsty,' I knew I had seen him somewhere before.

As I searched my memory, Rory Montagu, now fortified by a glass of gin and tonic, remarked, 'Well, good old Charlie! I can tell you it feels grand to get back to civilisation – don't know what I'd do without him! When did you come out?'

He was speaking to me. For a moment I stared at him with total incomprehension. Then I said automatically, 'Over.'

'I'm sorry?' He squinted at me in surprise.

'Not at all. It's just that we say "When did you come over?" in Ulster, and "out" sounds rather peculiar – you know, as if we were a colony on the other side of the globe? You'll pick up these things . . .' But he wouldn't, I knew, and I wished I had never started. Attempting to make amends, I went on, 'They must be a great strain, these tours you do on the border.'

He said grimly, 'Well, it's no picnic. You can't relax for a minute or trust a soul down there. You just look on the lot as terrorists, it's the only way to survive it. Of course, our chaps are terrific, but it makes you sick to see them sent out here to be slaughtered. It's high time . . .'

Bill Lamont interrupted him. 'It's high time the Government realised that it is *our* Government too, and is there to protect our interests and not to treat with the enemy. And the Army is *our* Army. What's it for, if not to fight for the liberty of its citizens? Not one of you is conscripted: you chose your job like I chose my job, and part of yours is to defend the constitution of this land by the use of arms where necessary.'

Olivia Glencreagh said coldly, 'I'm afraid I don't see it as necessary. Neither side has the least intention of trying to work out a way towards a reasonable compromise. No political initiative has been given a chance. And it seems to me that quite enough servicemen have gone to their deaths in Ireland . . .'

Bill Lamont cut in again, with one hand held aloft. 'Pardon me, if you please! We're not talking about Ireland. Ireland is another country, and I don't know about you, but I've no desire to visit it. We are talking about Ulster. And speaking as an Ulsterman, I have as much right as you, or any one in Britain, to protection from foreign aggression, be it cloaked as terrorism or not.'

I knew where I had seen him then. He had put Jim up for

adoption when he stood as a D.U.P. candidate, and had come to lunch at Dunvarden together with Heather and Jim, when I was paying a visit to my parents a number of years ago. In an effort to change the subject, I recalled the occasion to him, and saw too late that this ranged me on his side as a fellow Loyalist, though as a red herring it did its work well.

'For goodness sake!' he said. 'I've been taking you for a stranger – and you Jimmy McMurtry's sister!' The formality and stiffness that lunching with Lord Glencreagh had brought to his voice and manner had thawed into genuine pleasure, and he looked and sounded quite different. 'I've a great respect for Jim – a smart lad, we could do with more like him. I well remember meeting you, and your mother and your father too.' His face suddenly grew grave, 'But you've had some trouble, I understand. I was more than sorry to hear of it. I'm sure your poor father is very distressed.'

'My father's a stout-hearted man,' I said firmly. 'No terrorist blackmail is going to break his spirit. If he goes, he'll go down fighting.'

I assumed he was bound to know of my father's political attitude, but it seemed he had forgotten it, for he answered reassuringly, 'Well, no man need fight alone. Your father has a good son in Jim, and Jimmy's well supported. McMurtry's is a fine old firm, and even in Killycreel we're more than a match for the Catholics so long as we stick together. United we stand.' He paused and glanced up at Rory Montagu. 'There'd be fewer British soldiers killed if your government stood behind you, and allowed you to defend yourselves as you are trained to do, instead of signing treaties with the ones that are pledged to destroy us. We know what it's like to be frightened, son. Civilians are dying too, and more than enough in the UDR. But it's not just our lives that's threatened, it's our heritage and our future. When you go to Killycreel, you go there with the shadow of fear in your heart, and the Lord knows, I don't blame you – but for the likes of Alison here, that same place is her family home!'

There was a brief awkward silence, and then Sally exclaimed brightly, 'Oh, isn't that rather gloomy? Look at the wonderful way people cope with the situation and get on with their lives – well, almost as if nothing was happening at all! And such hospitality! I mean, we've been asked all over the place, thanks to Charlie and Olivia. It's such a beautiful country. We've been through Killycreel on our way down south, and never have I seen such a perfect setting! We stopped at the arboretum there – it's run by the Forestry, so of course you'll know all about it . . .' she smiled at Bill Lamont hopefully but, dismayed by his unresponsive face, turned back to Rory and me. 'Rory should go there sometime, shouldn't he? In the Spring. You'll still be here, won't you?' But Rory's expression was stony too.

'I'm afraid that Killycreel is out of bounds for the Army,' he said, 'that is, when we're off duty. It's not got a happy record for us, and speaking personally, I don't have any difficulty in steering pretty clear of it.' His knuckles showed white round his tumbler of gin, and I knew that he wanted to say 'It's a godforsaken neck of the woods, full of treachery and danger, and the very name makes me angry . . .' but good manners stood in the way of such an explosion of honesty, and instead he fixed one eye on me, while the other scampered round the room as if seeking some escape from the whole unfortunate topic.

He was saved by Charlie Glencreagh, who came up and patted him on the back. 'What's this? What's he steering clear of? Not girls, I suspect, nor whiskey?' Everybody laughed thankfully, except Bill Lamont who stared straight ahead with the disgusted expression of someone who wishes to distance himself from unseemly frivolity.

I thought of the years that my father had spent striving for some measure of harmony, and of the enormous gulf that lay between his Killycreel and the concepts of all these people. I looked from Olivia Glencreagh who felt that the obdurate should be left to fashion their own destruction instead of the murder of civilised men, past Bill Lamont standing at bay in defence of his Protestant birthright, to Rory who feared for his life in a land of barbarous fanatics; and finally at Sally, who understood nothing whatever – and my good spirits ebbed away and I longed, selfishly, to be free of the place, to be simply Alison Lacey, Charlie's picture expert from London, going back to Robin and Ben with a few good stories to illustrate the extent of Ulster's intransigence, and a job well done behind me.

Dejected, I turned away and stared out of the window. I felt profoundly useless. Those not with you are against you: the fact that I always could see, and never could help condemning, the innate sectarian bigotry behind every opinion and judgment only made my loyalty to my family a worthless thing – despite the long years of argument it had had no positive outcome. Even the real empathy I had always enjoyed with my father had been damaged by my rejection of the standards he took for granted. His own daughter! Where was she? The child he had bounced upon his knee in the family pew of a Sunday when she was an innocent baby? The girl who had promised to be such a credit, as chaste and Godfearing as any in the six counties? By the code of his circle, she'd gone to the bad . . . Many men less loving than he would have spurred the family on to disown such a disappointing offspring: instead he had struggled to keep the peace and had always welcomed me as if he were pleased to see me. But I had not brought him happiness, and there seemed little hope I could comfort him now. Although I was sickened to see his good faith betrayed and his principles dragged into open conflict with Jimmy's, my backing could only discredit his views.

The thought of Killycreel and its crazy ideologies had distressed but never frightened me, but suddenly it *was* frightening. I shrank from having to see my brother at war with my father, and my mother torn between them, and from facing the fact that as things stood now I had very good reason to be afraid for their physical safety as well as for their happiness. Yet I could do nothing for them – it was like being in a nightmare, I was caught and I was powerless, unable to speak or to flee. And as if to confirm the nightmare's hold, the flat Antrim horizon wavered, and superimposed upon it, as it would always be when I least desired to see it, lay the view from my room at Dunvarden: the lough calm, the hills bright with sunshine, the sky an innocent blue, and the houses tucked under the mountains's wing like eggs beneath a chicken, as harmless and charming a little town as a dreamer could wish to see.

That was just how it looked the next morning when we went down the hillside to collect my father from hospital – a cheerful and sparkling day, washed clean by the rain that had fallen all night and purged of evil and ugliness. My mother was tense with excitement. Her face was strained and pale, and she sat very upright beside me on the fat leather seat of the Rover. The Rover was my father's car, a large distinguished affair designed to last a lifetime and already of many years' standing, but my mother would never drive it; she managed to imply without actually putting it into words, that it was a man's prerogative to control such a powerful vehicle, and that she herself anyway was too lady-like and fragile to be trusted behind the steering-wheel. Today this stance had caused trouble, for the same standards proclaimed that the Rover was the only car in which Father could leave the Infirmary with the dignity due to his status.

'I'll ring Jim,' my mother had said, 'and ask him to come up and fetch the big car; Daddy would be much more comfortable, what with his poor head and everything. The Rover's properly sprung, and the road has got into a shocking state.'

We had not yet started breakfast, and the night had been bad. I said testily, 'Why on earth should you bother Jim? You know that he's up to the eyes as it is, and he's coming this evening anyway. I thought *we* were collecting Daddy.'

My mother's lips compressed with reciprocal irritation. 'Yes, dear. That *is* what I said, but then I thought that the Rover would really be much more suitable for bringing him home than that wee car of mine.'

'Well then, take the Rover!' I said. 'I don't see where Jimmy comes into it. Or we'll go in my car if you'd rather . . .' This was not an idea that she welcomed, and her face set obstinately, increasing my bad temper. 'Why make such a fuss about nothing? You're a perfectly capable driver – a better one than Jim. And besides I'm here now, what's the matter with me?'

She frowned. 'Nothing's wrong with you, Alison. It's just that I find the Rover is much too heavy for me. It's always been your father's car.'

'Right,' I said, 'and today I'm his chauffeur – we will cut a great dash when we get to the Moy . . . Why are you scrambling eggs? You know I don't eat a cooked breakfast.'

I saw her shoulders sag, and at once was ashamed of my victory. Invariably I despise myself when I find that I have won some petty point in our wranglings. Why hadn't I let her ring Jim? It would not have mattered to me and it might have made her feel better. It was probably true that she needed him more for the moral support that he gave than for his skill at driving. Maybe that was what I resented? At least he was coming to supper. I would have to make amends by seeing that the evening meal was the happy celebration for which she was hoping so fervently.

87

I had eaten the scrambled eggs and the beautifully grilled bacon as my first act of contrition. She had been on the defensive by then, and I had had to beg to be allowed to do so, but that had been part of my penance and had soothed her wounded feelings. Now tension had built up again as we drew closer to the Infirmary. I knew she was afraid I would spoil the send-off the Moy had prepared in honour of my father. It would be an emotive occasion, and the wrong remark carelessly made would shatter the feeling of unity so essential to her survival. I promised myself that on no account would I be provoked to say anything that would hurt her further.

Our reception fulfilled expectations: the Moy was making the most of us – it was not every day that it had the opportunity to care for its founder's descendants. Besides Father was twice a hero: he carried the family name and he had survived the terrorist. Enormous respect was due to him, and his undemanding good nature meant that this respect was paid with real warmth. Cleaners vied for the privilege of bringing him little comforts, the nurses were charmed by his obvious wish not to take up too much of their time, and, as a result, spent long hours in his room discussing their lives and their families; Matron was secretly flattered that he had refused the bed his consultant had offered to find for him down at the County General.

'We're all of us going to miss him,' she took my mother's hand. 'A real gentleman, that's what he is. I can tell you, Mrs McMurtry, there's not many left like your husband – and to think of him nearly dead at the hands of those monsters, for monsters they are!' Blue cotton and white starch crackled. 'Praise the Good Lord for watching over him!' Above her immaculate breast, grey hair and pink face and winged spectacles looked as if they too had been laundered. My mother knew her slightly, for they both had been born again, and met each other from time to time at gospel revivalist meetings. But whereas on these occasions Matron would have been proud to claim my mother's acquaintance, today it was she who felt honoured by Matron's attention and, as we clattered behind her up the polished marble stair and along the Victorian corridors where the walls were tiled up to our shoulders, we became the cynosure of all eyes. Ward sisters looked up from their desks and nurses peered from doorways, two orderlies wheeling a trolley became jammed in the door of the sluice room in their efforts to clear our path, and the clink of teacups could be heard, following at a respectful distance.

We found Father ready and waiting for us, very neatly groomed and dressed, as if for the office, in grey suit and tie. He stood up as we opened the door, despite Matron's attempt to restrain him ('Sit you there now, Mr McMurtry, Don't you trouble yourself to rise for us') and I knew he had made up his mind to overrule anybody who still treated him as an invalid. The dressing on his temple and the yellowing black eye and the way he had temporarily shrunk in his clothes must simply be disregarded. While preserving the most perfect courtesy, he would henceforth remain deaf and blind to all efforts to take control of him.

He saw Mother into a chair and Matron perched on the edge of the bed as meek as any schoolgirl, before he himself resumed his seat. I was allowed to stand for the purpose of pouring out the tea and handing round the biscuits, but there was no doubt about who was the host. As lately as yesterday, the tea party would have been Matron's, and my father 'poor Mr McMurtry', a babe in the hands of three women. Now 'poor Mr McMurtry' was gone, and authority restored again to its right and proper quarters. As I looked at his gentle determined face. I wondered whether Jim had ever appreciated the strength of his father's will and conviction; it is easy to underestimate an opponent in whose eyes you have always been a beloved son; but Father was stronger than Jimmy, I was sure of that. Only treachery would be able to undermine his particular brand of confidence, for in terms of trust he was vulnerable. Despite his adherence to Church and Faith, I knew he depended more on an ardent belief that goodness would triumph in human nature, than on any religious dogma. It was in that belief he had tried, with such patience and optimism, to stem sectarian friction – in his home, in his firm and in Killycreel. He had always recognised the threat posed by evil, but it was trust that gave him the strength and the courage to ignore the taboos of his colleagues. If that trust were to prove misplaced now, I feared it would break his spirit.

I turned aside hastily in case he might read the concern in my face, and found myself staring down at the Old Town beneath the Infirmary gates. The view is exceptionally fine from Moygarriff Hill, and it was once a popular subject for artists. At the time the Infirmary had been built, one canvas could combine both the triumph of modern technology and the fashion-appeal of a beauty spot, and this sold well to Ulster's industrialists. The amazing new canals themselves were a source of proper pride, but in such an idyllic setting, beneath those improbably lovely hills, progress seemed doubly blessed, as if ratified by the Almighty. The print above Father's desk was a typical example, sketched from just the same point on the hillside as the one on which I was standing now.

Since then, many things have changed. The New Town has blocked out the view of the sea, the dead gasworks obscures the harbour, the foothills are covered with bungalows. Across the estuary, where the print shows marshy pasture and a scattering of cottages, the huge drainage scheme built to extend the port has swept the old shoreline away and the main Dublin Belfast railway-line now runs through the empty dockland. But foreground and background have not changed at all. The tops of the mountains rise, free and wild above the houses. Like all Irish countryside, they carry an air of insolent resistance to human influence. They have not been subjugated. By contrast, English land is more docile, more domestic, content to be intertwined with the lives of those who care for it. You do not feel this in Ireland: man and earth are not in harmony. The proverbial 'hunger for land' is real enough, but savage. It has not given rise to partnership but a sense of ongoing conflict, oppressor and oppressed, with no love lost between them. The country rejects its history, it remains pristine, rudimentary, as sullen and untamed as any wildcat in a cage. No one has ever possessed its elemental spirit. No one will ever stand on Dunvarden Moor and feel the warmth given back by years of good husbandry, or enjoy that sense of belonging found where men are laid to rest in ground happy to receive them home. Its beauty is prehistoric. And the bones of the ruined cottages, like the runes on the dolmen stone, are mere scratches on the surface of its vast primordial indifference. If you love it, then you must love it for this.

Looking over the street below, I did not feel particularly loving. I felt trapped and exploited, a prisoner in a miserable place where attitudes never changed except to grow more inflexible. Why did I care for them – the unresponsive mountains, the mean little town that grew steadily uglier every year and had now tried to murder my father? Bitterness had long since stifled the charm that had lain in the road that ran under this window. The New Town might strike me as hideous, but the people of Killycreel disparaged only the Old Town. No local inhabitant would look at this pitifully neglected hill and find its buildings delightful, that was the privilege of an educated outsider, a Charlie Glencreagh, an Andrew or Sally Burleigh-Hall; even my father shook his head when he thought of the Old Town. It was no use, he said, putting money into repairing a lot of outdated buildings, he'd seen pigs better housed ... Irish cottages may still look exceptionally well on the pages of tourist brochures, or in pottery reproduction on the shelves of the airport gift shop, but in reality all Irishmen hurry to pull them down and build themselves a bungalow as soon as they can afford one. It was only poverty, not love, that had spared the street below, and it was sentimental to regard it as something precious: whatever it meant to me, it was squalid and uncherished. Rubbish floated in the gutters. A group of youths lounged round the horse trough. At the corner of the road, where it widened into the cobbled square, P. Flaherty, Wholesale Poulterer, was unloading a lorry of chicken crates. Several patients from what is known as 'the Mental', the Moy's psychiatric wing, were gesticulating around it, enthralled by its terrified cargo. In order to unload, the lorry had swung out across the square with its broadside against the building, and its cab stuck out into the street that led to the level-crossing below. This left room for an average car to squeeze past if it did not mind mounting the pavement, but there was little traffic. The driver was taking his time over the delivery of the birds; after all, it was a fine morning, and the monumental mason in the next premises but one was obviously an old friend of his. From my vantage point at the window I could see them enjoying a comfortable yarn in the yard behind the high wall among the urns and headstones.

I also noticed another thing no one on the ground could see – a convoy of Army vehicles, two Ferret scout cars and a Saracen, driving over the bridge and the railway-line, and beginning to climb the hill. As they left the level-crossing behind, its lights began to flash amber, and by the time the commander in the leading Ferret could see the delivery lorry across his path, the barrier had fallen.

The whine of the big armoured-personnel truck in low gear on the hill alerted the boys who were whiling away their empty day round the horse trough. They had been splashing each other and whistling hopefully at a handful of young nurses passing by on their way to the hospital, but the sight of the Ferret transformed them. Erupting suddenly in that atmosphere of good-humoured sloth, its appearance was physically shocking. Its wide snout and belligerent turret, the barrel of its gun, the sound of the Saracen close behind, all electrified the senses. It is never very pleasant to be faced unexpectedly by the mouth of a machine-gun, but the horror is stimulating. Until that moment, the boys in the square had been loitering harmlessly, dispirited by their own boredom, but now they were charged with energy, and the energy made them look purposeful. What the Ferret commander could see was a road blocked against his passage by a hefty delivery lorry, and a gang of youths gathering behind it, radiating hostility. What the boys saw was an aggressor, lethal, foreign, intensely insulting, making mockery of their manhood and their nationality.

For a minute the scene remained static as a frame held in a projector, a photograph in a paper. Then the man behind the gun spoke rapidly into his radio, no doubt suggesting withdrawal. Confrontation was against orders unless strictly necessary, and the roadblock might be accidental, he could try another side street. The reply from his rear changed this picture. The barrier down the hill was now firmly in position and the signal hung limply beside it in readiness for the Belfast express. It was not possible to retreat and, if this were another booby trap, a bomb might go off any second; the stage was well set for massacre. With a polite restraint that did him much credit, he hailed the square and asked for the road to be opened.

'Will the driver of the lorry SIJ 6761 move his vehicle immediately? It is causing an obstruction. Will the driver of the lorry SIJ 6761 . . .?'

Behind him, men streamed from the Saracen and dropped to one knee on the pavements. Helmets and combat jackets. Young faces made ugly with dread. Minds filled with past atrocities. Hands clutching self-loading rifles. They dare not touch the lorry. If you were seeking death, that was the first place you would look for it. Yet meanwhile they were helpless. The platoon was a sitting target for a terrorist attack, a planted bomb, or a sniper's fire from the shabby houses above them.

'Get a bloody move on, will you? Shift that lorry off the road!'

The voice rose: fear had won its battle for control of the loud hailer, and the boys ducked behind the horse trough. Shame was preferable to death, but if only they had a rock or two, or a crate of empty bottles, they'd have flung them at those buggers with their rifles and combat dress! Boys of their own age and younger, strutting round as if they owned the place, as if Irishmen were worthless scum, despised and dispossessed. How they loathed them! How they envied them their arrogance and their uniform! How they longed to avenge the indignity that they were suffering today, that they would continue to suffer in the long unemployed tomorrows.

'Go home, youse fucking English gits . . .'

Old Phelim Flaherty appeared in the door of his warehouse and peeked round the back of his chicken crates. Holy Jesus, the Brits were attacking! And the driver – where would he be? Slumped dead in his cab already perhaps? He drew his head back abruptly, but he did not scuttle for cover, for out there he could see the five patients from the Mental, still giggling and pointing, unaware they would soon be mown down like corn. Dear Blessed Mother of God, the poor simpletons! It was terrible! Well, he'd never been known for his courage and

94

he might be stone deaf, but he still had his eyes, and he'd not stand here helplessly and see murder done ... With startling speed for one so aged and arthritic, he secured his place in heaven by dashing out into the square and shepherding the five lunatics to the safety of his premises. The big doors rolled shut behind them.

It was now, somewhat tardily, that the driver decided to break off his chat with his kinsman, and bow to pressure. He knew that his lorry was blocking the street. He was not remotely deaf, and he had heard the loud hailer as he leaned on a granite headstone and discussed his racing pigeons. The one thing he did not know was the fact that the level-crossing was shut. Bloody Brits, he'd see them in hell before he would put himself out for them! Let them bawl away out there – if they didn't like the waiting, they could back down the hill to the main street. But even behind the stone wall of the yard, the atmosphere in the square and the undertone of panic in the voice that was shouting instructions, began to make themselves felt to him. With those bastards you never could tell, and if they blew up his lorry, he'd look a right eejit, wouldn't he, resting here among the gravestones? He bid a reluctant farewell to the monumental mason, and stepped into the arena.

I had not recognised him earlier, for his face had been turned away from me, and yet when I saw it was Colm, it came as no surprise; I suppose, even from the back, his stance had jogged my recollection. Now I watched him walk, insolent and calm, towards the kneeling men, apparently oblivious to the Ferret's mounted machine-gun, and the dozen pointing rifles. The handful of boys were still there, cowering underneath the horse trough. As he passed, he spoke one curt word that brought them on to their feet as fast as if they had been stung by a scorpion, and when he reached his empty cab he spat deliberately towards the platoon of soldiers. I wondered if they knew then, as I did, that his was the only true hate that they had encountered that morning? Almost certainly not. Far more probably, like Rory Montagu, they felt that they had been facing a horde of vicious assassins. How could they dare to think otherwise? The tragedy of the thing was that their very presence could not fail to rouse animosity and fresh sympathy for the terrorist cause. They had behaved perfectly, yet their conduct had stirred up feelings of resentment and aggression that were absent only a moment before. Even Phelim Flaherty, no doubt by now surrounded by admiring relations and workers, would have a bloodcurdling tale to relate; each and every family of the handicapped patients would thank him for his deed of heroism, overlooking the fact that no shots had been fired and no impropriety committed by the soldiers. Worst of all, the boys in the square had felt themselves affronted; they had been humiliated, made to look abject and ridiculous in the middle of their own town by an alien force of warriors armed and clothed for deadly battle. The insult and the shame of it, the fear – and under it all, the addictive thrill of danger, would remain a vivid experience, and because it was so personal would do a great deal more to secure support for the IRA than the best Sinn Fein propaganda.

And Colm – how often since Colm had been forced to face up to the heavies for playing on his harmonica on a sunny afternoon instead of remaining silent in the presence of his betters – how often had *his* pride been mortified? How unfairly and frequently had he been singled out at roadblocks? Personality checked on the side streets? 'Lifted', taken in for questioning? How long can anyone with nothing but his own wits to pit against discrimination and military strength, remain free from hate? At least it was good to see that he had a job. Maybe that would help to keep him out of real trouble.

I became aware that my father was standing near to me

and looking over my shoulder. Colm was reversing his lorry. The soldiers were back in the Saracen and the youths, wild with impotent rage, were shouting obscenities after them as they bumped away over the cobbles. Their cries drifted up to the window and my mother exclaimed with distaste, 'What on earth's going on there, Carson? There's an awful lot of commotion.'

My father shook his head wearily. 'It's nothing really,' he said, 'just the Army on one of their patrols, and a few lads taking exception. They got a bit stuck in the traffic, but they seem to be on their way. No harm done.'

'It's disgusting,' said Matron. 'Just listen to that language! My nurses are always complaining they can't walk up the hill without a crowd of those lazy good-for-nothings shouting after them. And we give them the dole! Those rebels! Loyal people working away and paying their taxes so ruffians like that can hang round abusing the Army! I tell you, I'd give them nothing. If they want to behave that way, let them draw their dole over the border, and see how they like what they get there! The devil finds work for idle hands.'

'Well, they can't help their idleness,' my father exclaimed. 'There's no work for them here . . .'

My mother intervened quickly, 'Carson dear, you've been up on your feet far too long. will you not sit and drink your tea? You'll be tired before we've got started.'

Our eyes met and held for a moment, and I saw she knew very well that the one sure way to deflect my father's thoughts from unemployment was to question the strength of his stamina. This trick was familiar to me, and I found myself smiling with her as he took the bait. 'Well Noreen, I'll not say no to the tea, but there's nothing wrong with my legs, you know, and I'm looking forward to using them. I think I'll go out this afternoon . . .'

We left the Moy regally, with much hand-shaking and

waving. Matron embraced my mother. Sister gave my father a parcel which later turned out to be a book of collected sermons by American evangelists, one of whom was a relation of hers. Junior staff clustered eagerly behind the leading characters and added their words of encouragement.

'You're not beat yet, Mr McMurtry, dear!'

'The Lord watch over ye – these are difficult times!'

'Keep your spirits up – we'll win if we stick together.'

'We'll be praying for you and your family.'

My mother gave Nurse Magee the large box of chocolates that she had brought as a present for the ward staff and I knew that she chose her deliberately to show that the family did not hold her accountable for the fact that her sort were behind the outrage. (Carson spoke so highly of her, poor little Nurse Magee! You'd not think that she was a Catholic at all if it weren't for the look of her.)

I went and fetched the Rover, and we tucked Father comfortably into the front seat, with a rug on his knees. As my mother got in behind us there were tears in her eyes, and she blew her nose hard.

'Such wonderful people,' she said. 'They've been wonderful, haven't they, Carson? Such a help and support in our troubles.' She paused and then added defensively, 'No matter what they say about us over the water, there's no better place to be living. Where else would you find such loyalty? I'm beginning to think nowadays that maybe Jim's right, and that we could defeat all this evil and terrorism if we could just run our own Province. If they'd put a few people away in this town for a start, I'd sleep sounder myself. And we don't need to look far to find them.'

As she finished, we reached the first ridge of the hill, and before either of us could answer, we had turned towards Dunvarden, and the moor and the hills and the sea lay before us, drained of their blues and greens, and literally sparkling like metal beneath the big colourless disc of the sun.

Father said spontaneously, 'Did you ever see anything like it?' and I stopped the car for a moment, and we sat and stared at the gold and grey till the sun shining into our eyes made us turn away dazzled. For that short time the love between us was simple, as warm and uncomplicated as it had been when I was a child.

My mother had gone to great trouble in preparing our meal that evening. On account of Jimmy's children, she agreed reluctantly that it should be served around six o'clock. 'Of course, I had planned to eat later, but Heather says they will be starving . . .'

'So will I,' my father said. 'I've never got used to this non-sense of waiting to fill your stomach until you're about to go up to your bed. It makes no sense to me, and it gives me indigestion. But then I'm a humble mortal, no blue blood in my veins, eh Alison?' he winked at me jovially, and then laid his hand on my mother's arm and patted it with affection. 'Don't put on your airs for Alison. She may eat with Lord Glencreagh at every kind of outlandish hour, but this is the house she was reared in and she'll not be expecting a midnight feast. Six o'clock will do very well. And a cup of tea later, before they go home.'

Jim and Heather arrived very promptly, with Ian and Ruth in their best party clothes. They were clearly determined to be as convivial as was possible in a difficult situation. I had not seen Heather since Father was hurt, and she greeted me hesitantly with a kiss timed too late to avoid awkwardness, and yet obviously meant to show sympathy. Underneath the bright smile, she looked anxious and tired. For the first time I wondered if she disliked and deplored me as much as I thought, or whether she just found me baffling. We had little enough in common, and an opportunity to get to know each other well had not arisen naturally, or perhaps we had not cared to find one. My relationship with Jim had been at its nadir around the time that Heather joined the family, for I too had announced my engagement, and in Jim's eyes that had been a decision so stunning and scandalous that he hardly could bear to look at me, let alone stage a meeting between us. It was only my father's distress that had driven me to his wedding at all, and then I had gone grudgingly, sour with anger and resentment – feelings perfectly matched by Jim's own attitude towards me as a renegade to his principles, and a source of shame to his people. As a start, this naturally did not waken warm sisterly feelings between myself and Heather, and, although we had never quarrelled, and our kinship had gradually forged some kind of bond between us, we had never established a friendship.

Now, watching my mother in action, it struck me forcibly that her habit of publicly stressing the differences between us had made real affection impossible; apart from annoying me (as it was plainly designed to do, for the contrasts all favoured Heather), it reduced her too to confusion – she had not chosen to be seen as a model of perfection. Tonight she looked miserably flustered as my mother sailed into the attack, remarking pointedly, 'I'm so glad you're early, Heather. Alison has no interest in cooking and I do love some help when it comes to the food;' she glanced across at me with a sort of sad triumph, 'a little advice, that's all. Just a bit of encouragement.'

'Oh, I'm sure that Alison . . .' Heather began, but my mother waved her hand. 'I'm afraid Alison is no housewife. She's too busy looking at pictures,' she put her arm round her small grand-daughter's waist, 'though I always say, Ruthie child, it would be a dull world if we all were the same, and you're Granny's help, aren't you my darling?'

Ruthie smiled the calm smile of a putative cook, but Heather turned to me in an effort to change the subject, 'Isn't

Grandad simply wonderful? Home from hospital, and up and about!' She lowered her voice intimately, 'I mean, Jimmy and I were so worried. At his age, you know: not just the injuries, but the shock of it all can be terrible ... Well, I daresay no one can tell how the elderly will get over these things, but I must say he's surprised us! I just hope he'll take things easy now and lean a bit more on Jim. Old folks always find it so difficult to accept they can't cope any longer.'

I fought with my irritation. 'But he's only sixty-three! I can think of a dozen heads-of-state who are as old, or older, and manage to cope quite capably. I hardly think that Jim need worry about that for some years to come.' I smiled, I hoped reassuringly and not with downright condescension 'I'm sure he'll be right as rain in a week or two – won't you, Daddy?' for he had come up to join us. 'I was just going to stake my money that you would be beating Jim on the golf course before winter's over.' For twenty years he and Jim had been members of the same golf club, and their competitions were famous.

Now Jimmy laughed and said ruefully, 'And no one will rout for Jim because he's not been in hospital. Some people get all the attention! Maybe I could look out a few bandages ...'

My mother cried, 'Shame on you, Jim! That's no subject to start making jokes about!' But in fact, she too was smiling, and suddenly we were united, an ordinary family trying hard to make light of a narrow escape that could have ended in tragedy.

This mood was so strong that it even survived my father revealing that he had opened a bottle of excellent wine. 'You'll join me, won't you, Alison? I'll not drink alone, but your Mummy's good food is deserving of more than water.'

Since my mother and Jimmy have taken the pledge, this remark would normally have provoked much disapproval and warning looks at the children, until my unfortunate father was moved to retorting truculently, as he had a score of times before, 'Well, I'm sorry if it offends you, but we know the Lord Jesus Himself took a glass, and that's good enough for me!' But today the solidarity that had suddenly come upon us bore us through the critical moment, and my mother only said 'Ach, Carson . . .' in tones you might use to a child, and went out to fetch the fruit cup.

At the table grace was said, brief and to the point, by my father. 'Of Your mercy may You bless this food to our use, as You bless our lives to Your eternal service.' Ruth and Ian exchanged glances. Extemporary graces were said in Jim's house, and on special occasions they could last for several minutes, never mind that your soup was congealing. Maybe if Grandad said longer graces and didn't drink liquor, the Lord would protect him better from the wickedness of the Catholics . . .

Heather, still trying hard to please, enquired about Robin. 'It seems a long time since you brought him over, Alison. We should get the young ones together.'

This was touching hazardous ground. I had brought Robin to Dunvarden quite a lot when he was little, but my repeated suggestions that Jim's children should visit me and see the sights in London had been turned down without explanation, and indeed I did not need one. I had no doubt that Heather and Jim would as soon have sent their children off to Sodom or Gomorrah, as expose them to the perils of staying with Ben and me in a household where sin openly replaced the sanctity of wedlock. Besides Robin, as his father's son, obviously could never be anything but an acute embarrassment as an acknowledged cousin, and the less seen of him the better.

That we both were well aware of this delicate situation, made poor Heather's remark less than tactful, and I saw she regretted the blunder. The illusion of friendship lay in mortal danger between us and I did my best to rescue it. 'Yes, we

102

must make an effort – time goes by so fast. My goodness, look at the size of your two these days! They'll be grown up and gone before we know what's happening.'

'Gone where?' interjected Ian, putting down his fork with a clatter, 'I tell you, I'm going no place!' His voice was indignant and shrill, and Heather frowned at him reproachfully, but Jimmy cried, 'Well spoken, son! Why go stravaiging round the world when you've a home to rest in? Roaming never brought anyone wisdom.'

'Away out of that with you, Jim,' said my father rather sharply. 'Don't you fill the child's head with such nonsense. There's a lot wrong with this Province that the likes of you and me might have rectified a long time ago if we'd had a wider perspective. Travelling broadens the mind . . .'

Jim's face darkened, and he cut in angrily, 'If by "broadens" you mean corrupts it, then perhaps I would agree with you. You just look across the water, Pop, and tell me – what do you see? Empty churches. Moral degeneracy. Marriage, as we know it, meaningless. No community spirit. No family love. Old folks thrown out of their homes – if homes you could call them! Vice walking the streets. Drugs, drink, crime, prostitution . . .'

'James, please! Remember the children!'

Jimmy turned incredulously, and glared at his wife. 'The children! Has the Lord saved you and me from the path of sin so that we should allow our own children to be corrupted? How will they know what corruption is, if all that they can see is their parents excusing iniquity on the grounds that it is "broad-minded"? Weak-minded more like! Why, the path to Hell is as broad as it can be! It's the narrow path we must follow. And it's here,' he smote his breast, 'it is here in our hearts we will find it. In our homes. In our own country. In the salvation of our people from depravity and wickedness. Where else need we look for a challenge?'

My father half-humorously rapped the bowl of his spoon on the table. 'That's enough for the moment, Jimmy! No doubt you'd make a great preacher, but a little civility will do us nicely just now, I think. Ruthie, please pass your aunt the potatoes.' He glanced round our uneasy faces. 'Well, it's very nice to see all my family around me. It's a shame that young Robin's not with us.' He smiled at me rather anxiously, and I knew he was thinking of Ben, who in fact had been under a covert attack. Ben works for the BBC, and is an inveterate traveller who directs documentary films renowned for their objectivity. But desire to acknowledge Ben as a part of his family circle now vied with his other loyalties. Poor Noreen had gone to such trouble; he had a duty to see that this meal went as smoothly as possible. A reference to Ben would simply spur Jim to renew his crusade . . .

As it happened, the logic that led to this decision was wasted, for another crusader was imminent. Ruth, observing her father's frustration, and having no fondness for me, seized upon the subject of Robin.

'Robin can't come here now,' she said. 'It's his ones that blew up Grandad. Daddy knows the Catholics well, and he says there's not one but would stab you in the back as soon as look at you. You're better not talking to them, you can't trust them unless they're dead. We don't want to have them ones about our house.'

A terrible stillness fell on the room as she finished speaking. Her high voice stabbed through the air and found a target in each of us. Jim's face shone hot and red; my father's paled. Heather's jaw fell agape. My mother pressed her hand across her mouth, as though hoping to stay her grand-daughter's lips by proxy. Our food lay forgotten before us. Ruthie, proud at having made such a sensible speech on her father's behalf, first looked round with satisfaction and then, as it dawned upon her that the sentiments she had expressed had misfired in some hideous manner, with a stare of growing bewilderment. My father was the first to speak.

'Jim, if your youngsters should say anything of this kind in my home again, I shall have to ask you to leave it. Alison has lost a husband, and is bringing up a son in the Catholic faith. I do not intend to have any of them insulted.'

'Ruthie didn't mean it,' said Heather. 'She just picks up what they say at the school, in the streets, all over the place . . .'

Ruth, finding herself betrayed as well as mysteriously disgraced, grew white with shock and resentment. Mummy knew, Daddy knew, what she'd said was the truth; how could they deny what they'd told her? How could Grandad defend the Catholics? Why, only yesterday Daddy'd said that there wasn't a Catholic but would sell your soul to the Romans – and whatever that meant, it was terrible. The Pope ruled over Rome, and surely everyone knew that he was wicked beyond redemption; that he worshipped dead people instead of the Lord, and that he gave orders to blow up Protestants like Grandad because they followed Jesus?

Her eyes narrowed. All this was Aunt Alison's fault. Why couldn't she stay in England? Mummy said that she had 'fallen', and that when people 'fell' you must always be kind. Well, she understood that, a fall could be very painful, and presumably Aunt Alison's had seriously injured her brain, like poor old Mrs Greer who had slipped on the stairs and ended up in the Mental. But today, suddenly, she wondered . . . Supposing Mummy had lied (as in a way she was doing now by concealing Daddy's opinions) – and Aunt Alison was just plain sinful? Grandad too? What if she should find that their souls had already been sold to Rome? The confusion was awful, frightening. Granny's lovely party was ruined; she feared she was going to cry with sheer rage and disappointment.

'Ruth,' she heard her mother say, 'you apologise to Aunt Alison! I've never seen such behaviour! I'm absolutely astonished at you – whatever made you say such cruel things about Robin? We all know that you don't mean them.'

Ruth sprang out of her chair. 'I do mean them!' Her voice rose to a yell, 'We don't want any dirty old Catholics here! You know rightly what Daddy said! He said they're all of them traitors, and that Wee Pat has tried to kill Grandad. You'd not know what Robin mightn't do.'

Sobs choked her. Her face, pinched and plain with misery and anger, her red hair struggling free from Heather's restraining bands and clips, her embattled stance by the sideboard, her stinging sense of injustice, brought the child I used to be so vividly before me that my desire to console her was almost a selfish emotion. Her words were too ordinary, too familiar in content, to touch me at all, but the manner in which she spoke them struck home like a blow to a half-healed wound. Her physical likeness to me was bad enough, but this sudden glimpse of a personality both as open to hurt, and as closed to the art of ingratiation as I was, made my sense of loss almost unbearable; yet the kinship and sympathy that I felt now, would be as unwelcome to her as the overtures of an enemy. Life had offered no Colm to Ruthie, and already I could see that it was too late; the ideas were formed, the love and allegiance given. You must find your Colm early. No school could have set me free had the mould not already been broken.

But what good were these thoughts to Ruthie? It was not my approval she looked for. I said, 'For heaven's sake, Jim, have the honesty to support the child! We all know it's your words she's repeating. The least you could do is admit it.'

My father's face was grim, and before Jim could answer, he intervened. 'Let's just clear up one point,' he said, 'for it's a serious matter.' He looked witheringly at Jim, as if the sight disgusted him. 'Am I to understand that you have been telling your daughter that Wee Patsy has tried to murder me? For that's a malicious falsehood! Do you hear me? A scandalous lie! It has no foundation whatever, and I'd thank you to retract it. I'll not stand for a man being slandered by any son of mine.'

He turned to Ruth and said gently, 'The people who nearly killed me are political terrorists, Ruthie. They are bad, ungodly men. No good Christian can be a terrorist – no good Catholic, and no good Protestant. If they claim to be either, they're telling a lie. Terrorism has nothing to do with Robin or Patsy Hourican, who are both of them Christian people, never mind of which persuasion. Robin is my own grandchild, like you. And Patsy,' he turned back to Jimmy, 'Patsy is my trusted employee. And if friendship means more than a social charade, then he is an old friend too.

'I am going to see him tomorrow,' he went on. 'Alison will take me. But it's not her place to visit him, and I'd thought of asking you to come down to the County with me instead – not just as a kindness to Patsy, but as a sign to the terrorist that the two of us still stand united in what we believe to be right.' He paused on the edge of the precipice; then he said with a heart-rending eagerness, 'So will you come with me, Jim? As a gesture of peace between us?'

I thought, nothing will mend this damage, for Jimmy will refuse him. In my anguish I turned aside and found myself facing Heather. Perhaps she could influence Jim; she was kind, she was fond of my father. But she had put up her hand to conceal her face, and her head was bowed. For a moment I thought she was praying, and then I observed the small neat tears that ran down beneath her palm and dripped off her chin. Yet even then I was not warned of what was coming, not even when I had steeled myself to glance at Jim, and found his face full of a pity of which I had deemed him incapable. He seemed to be quite at a loss for words.

107

At last he said, 'Look, I'm afraid something's happened, Pop. I must admit that I wasn't going to tell you, not tonight – but I just don't see how I can disguise it from you now the subject's come up between us. May the Lord forgive me if I am wrong.

'Wee Patsy,' he paused miserably, then went on with a rush, 'Wee Pat Hourican's dead. Jack McGuire phoned me from the hospital. He asked me to break it to you, for he knew you were bound to be extremely upset to hear it.' He leaned forward in great agitation, and burst out, 'Ah, Daddy – I'm sorry! It's true that there's grown up to be a wealth of difference between us these days, but I still hate to bring you bad tidings.'

He stopped, but my father said nothing. He was staring fixedly at the polished table, although it was plain that he did not see what was before him. My mother got up and went round to his chair. She put her hand hesitantly on the rigid curve of his shoulder, nervous of invading his privacy yet driven by instinct to do so, and after a little while he responded by covering it with his own.

He said dully, 'What way was he taken?'

'Apparently it was a haemorrhage on account of the head injury. He was out of the intensive care, but it seems that these things can happen. Jack McGuire said he didn't suffer at all.'

My mother said bitterly, 'Well, the ones that are responsible will suffer both here and in heaven.'

My father's eyes suddenly focused again, and he slowly raised his head. 'We are all responsible, Noreen. You. Me. Protestants and Catholics. We rear out children like heathens to despise their fellow men; we spawn preachers and polititions who have never learned humility.' He waved down Jim's interruption. 'Oh yes, on both sides, Jim, on both sides. And both should know better. The weak men who follow hate because they're afraid to resist it, would have no hate to follow if it was not fed by bigotry, bigotry that every day you and I condone by our silence or conspire to increase by our actions. We are all of us responsible, and will suffer for Patsy's death if there's justice in the hereafter.'

His voice was stern, almost menacing. Ruth had run round the table to Heather, and was now standing with her head buried in her mother's shoulder. Ian's face had gone white as mutton fat.

My mother cried, 'Carson, Carson! I know you're very distressed, but you're frightening the children. Why, you know that you're talking nonsense.'

My father gave no sign of hearing her. 'So Patsy's gone,' he said, speaking more to himself than to anyone else. 'And I never got to see him. Never bid him goodbye. After all this time . . .'

His voice gradually faded away, as though lost in the years that had vanished. Then he jerked himself out of his reverie. 'He was murdered in my service, and as God bears me witness,' he said, 'I will speak out against what has killed him. The one that struck the blow will be punished according to law, I don't doubt: he's already a soul lost to evil. But the evil itself – by my life that was spared when poor Patsy's was taken away, I swear I will fight the black prejudice that promotes that evil among us!'

As he flung down the gauntlet, his eyes fixed on Jim, and between them the sorrow and waste of the centuries spread like a shadow, a contagion wherein lay the death of their lifetime's shared trust and affection.

For a moment I watched them gaze, appalled, at the prospect before them; and then at last they faltered, with a visible effort clawed back from the brink. My father's eyelids fell, and he let his cheek rest on my mother's arm; and Jimmy, his face raw with stress, turned aside from the challenge pride

109

urged him to meet – two homely and principled men, struggling with an age-old conflict whose power was relentlessly weakening the bond of the loving relationship they both longed to enjoy again.

After supper we sat round the fireside and attempted to comfort each other. Jim discussed golf with my father, and took him tee by tee round a very significant match he had played just before the attack on the timber yard. My mother got out a new tapestry and politely consulted me on what colours it would be best to use. Heather chattered on doggedly about Ruthie's new dancing classes and the rising cost of groceries. On the floor behind the sofa, the children played bagatelle on the old board that once had been Jimmy's and mine. The tapping of the cue and the rumble and click of the metal balls as they rolled down the board was consoling. After all, we were still here together, needlework and bagatelle and golf were still part of our daily lives; Jim could still tell a funny story and my father could still laugh at it. Pat, stiff on his hospital bed, and the burned-out frames of the lorries in the gutted shed on the quayside must be pushed to the edge of our consciousness. Perhaps if we could deny the existence of friction and heartbreak, they would not engulf us completely. The children particularly seemed to feel this. Ruthie, now her tears were dry, laughed a good deal louder than usual. Ian treated the firing spring of the bagatelle board with a violence that exploded the balls round the woodwork without any regard for accuracy. They quarrelled noisily, but without ill-feeling, about the score.

At nine I went out to make tea, for my father was looking exhausted and the children were past their bedtime. As I turned from the sink with the kettle, I was startled to find that Jim had followed me into the kitchen and was hovering behind me. I jumped, splashing water all over the stove.

'Here, easy does it,' said Jim. 'I just wanted to have a quick word with you.'

I nodded, but we both fell silent, standing there rather awkwardly and watching the drops I had spilt on the hob hissing round on the scalding metal until the last one was extinguished. Then Jim said, 'I know you and me may not see things eye to eye, Alison, but no matter what our difference, I'm sure that Pop's welfare is close to our hearts. It would be a great help to me if you'd give me a hand to prevent him heading into serious trouble. Trouble that could well be avoided.'

His fixed gaze was disturbing me, and I went to the dresser and took down the cups in order to escape it. 'What kind of trouble exactly? There doesn't seem much I can do to prevent the kind of disaster that has landed him in hospital. And as far as policy matters go, it's my opinion that you have done more to stir up trouble for the firm since you sat as a Councillor than Daddy has done in a lifetime.'

Jim said coldly, 'I'm not asking you to interfere in policies, for you don't know the first thing about them. How could you, and you stuck in London? What I'm asking you to do is to keep him away from the Old Town just now – from that wee man's wake and funeral, from the whole stinking rat's nest of traitors. They're Provos, through and through, and there isn't a Loyalist in the place but would tell you the same story. It's not fitting that he should be seen up there.'

'Maybe that's how it looks to you,' I said, 'but that's not how he'll see it. The proper thing to do, the thing he'll regard right and fitting is to go up and visit the Houricans. He'll not rest till he's paid Pat his last respects.'

'Respects!' he spat back the word. 'Is it murderers now that are claiming respect?' The old Jim burst suddenly through the constraints of the saved Christian, 'Jesus Christ Almighty, Alison! Are you off your bap completely? Must I

111

spell it out for you? We're in danger of our lives up there! Pat Hourican is a traitor. He knew Pop was down at the works that night, but his son's in the IRA and he let him in with his firebombs – a killer, like all the rest of them. Pop's life didn't count a fig to him.'

'But it isn't Daddy who's dead,' I protested, 'it's Patsy Hourican! And why? Why did they attack him? If they'd wanted to make him look innocent, they'd have left him gagged and bound by the gates, where he would have been perfectly safe. If he was on their side, he'd have made up a pretty fanciful tale about who it was that assaulted him. If it happened as you are suggesting, he'd have been their best alibi.'

I offered these thoughts to Jimmy in the genuine hope of enlightenment. I had seen Colm's bearing that morning, and it had not disposed me to doubt Jim's assessment of his politics; yet I still could not reconcile a lethal attack upon Patsy with the theory that they were conspirators, and doubt made the whole outrage more horrible. If Jim could convincingly tie up the loose ends of the riddle, I was ready to believe him, and at least look the tragedy square in the face. The fear that flashed into his eyes was the last thing that I had bargained for.

'Don't you say such a thing!' he cried. 'Don't you dare to drag innocent men into this! Have we not all endured enough torment, without you spreading ignorant lies about something you don't know a blind thing about?' He grabbed me by the shoulder. 'There's no ifs and buts to it, Alison! Another man has died in another Republican attack, and it could have been your father. Next time – and there will be a next time, if we don't declare for our own and stop toadying to our enemies – he may not get off so lightly. That's what you should be concerned about, instead of wanting to know a whole lot of irrelevant details. Our boys have got nothing to hide, and anyone who suggests it . . . .'

112

'Just a minute! I did not suggest it.'

Jim shrugged off this statement impatiently. 'It was what your remark implied. And in case Pop is somewhat confused in his mind as well, let me tell you something – they're lifting Colm Hourican. It seems they've been waiting to see if he leads them to his accomplice. There's a good notion who he might be, but they're still a bit short on the evidence, and your boyo might just have provided it. But now that the charge is murder, Jo Baker's been telling me that they'll not hang around much longer.'

I said, 'So they do know it's Colm? They've got definite proof of that, anyway?'

Jimmy laughed. 'Oh, certainly! Fingerprints every place. On the bell. On the gate.' He relaxed. 'You'd not believe it. Leaving fingerprints on the security bell, and him in the IRA! Maybe he was afraid that he'd frighten his Da if he came with his hood and his gloves on!'

His mirth died. 'Well, Pat got his come-uppance. To be struck down by your own son! These are terrible times . . .' The saved Christian was back, both the fear and the triumph had faded. He went on, 'I'm sure you'll appreciate that what I've told you tonight is not to go any further. I hope it's made you see the necessity of persuading Pop that he's got to accept reality. Heaven knows, he's a powerfully obstinate man! He will pay no heed to me.'

Ian's head appeared round the door jamb. 'Grandad says have you both gone to India to pick the leaves from the bushes? What's happened to the tea?'

'It's coming right now. Here, you take the milk, it always spills on the trolley.'

As the child turned away and we moved to the door, I said hastily to Jim, 'I'll pass on the news if you want me to; he's got to know it anyway. But it's no good my telling him what to think. The best that I can do is to ask him to behave

113

prudently for all our sakes, specially Mummy's. But I wouldn't take bets on his listening to me.'

'You can wind him round your finger. You always could.' He was whispering now, facing me and walking backwards as we trundled the trolley across the hall, guiding it instinctively so its wheels would not stick where the stone flags were worn, and I thought of the countless evenings we had spent in this house together: secrets swapped in the privacy of the empty kitchen; mutual schemes for exploiting my father's indulgence – 'If you ask him, perhaps he'll let us'; early efforts to make tea and bring it in to our parents. What had happened to him, my brother? Why was nothing left between us? Where was all the old intimacy that should have sustained us through times like these? Gone, corrupted by the same plague that now crept between him and his father.

A great sense of futility, and a sadness I thought was long conquered made my eyes swim as, deft from long practice, we cleared the bump into the sitting room. Then I heard my mother say, 'You're for early bed after this, Carson dear,' and my father replying cheerfully, 'Well, I won't make a fuss for this evening. Tomorrow's another day,' and I felt ashamed. Here I was, sick at heart just because I had glimpsed a lost Jimmy who remembered the flaws on the floor of a hall, while my father faced the decay of everything that he had worked for with the fortitude of a stoic. It was no time to sanction nostalgia, and I hastily thrust it away.

My mother has formulated a solitary ritual which she plays out before she retires for the night. My father locks the door, stands the fireguard before the embers, makes sure that the lights are extinguished, and then says, 'Well, there we are, Noreen. I think that seems to be all. I'm away to my bed.'

'You go on, Carson dear. I'll be up in a wee jiffy.'

After that, though all help is steadfastly refused, you will hear her quick step on the floor below you for anything up to an hour. Setting things to rights, she calls it, and a small noble smile of endurance makes it plain that nothing more can be achieved by you lingering on; the process cannot be started until everyone else has succumbed to fatigue. That she is tired as well, but must suffer for others, is shown by the smile.

So when I had washed up the supper things, put away the bagatelle and plumped up the cushions, I bade her goodnight.

'Yes, you have a nice hot bath, darling. I'll be up when I've just set a few things to rights.' I was sorry to hear that the phrase had lost its ring of martyrdom, she was clearly too distraught to play her habitual character part with any sort of conviction. Instead, as I moved to the staircase, she suddenly exclaimed, 'We must do something for poor Daddy! He's not fit for all this agitation.' The words came in a rush of discomfiture. She had turned her head away as if to divorce herself from them. 'I'm at my wits' end about him. He needs a rest from the business, a bit of a holiday, a wee while away from Jimmy. They're too much on top of each other. You can see that it isn't good for them, working down there every day and squabbling over nothing. It's high time that he thought of retiring.'

I went back to her side in the sitting-room. 'He won't go abroad,' she said, 'not even on one of those package tours. He's always hated travelling. But he might visit you in London.'

'Well, that would be lovely,' I said. 'Both of you are always welcome to stay as long as you like with us.'

She let the 'us' pass without comment. 'If he could just get away, I'm sure he would feel quite different. He'd relax. He would see that Jimmy can manage quite well without him and has sensible things to say about steering the firm through these dangerous times.' She was twisting the rings on her fingers, staring down at her hands. 'Poor Carson. His ideas have had their day. There's no room for his moderate talk any more. It's turning our own ones against him. And the others have never listened to a word he's said anyway. But he's just too simple to see it, too simple and maybe too stubborn,' she looked up at me then with the ghost of a smile, 'like yourself.'

I smiled back at the sally, but the moment's accord undermined her control. She put her hands to her head, with her palms to her temples as though it might burst. 'All this talk of conciliation! In God's name, I am sick sore and tired of it! All this wondering what to do about the wants and wishes of the ones who blow us to pieces. Must we meet and treat with the Devil? What's this country coming to that we have to justify ourselves every time we act against evil?'

She sat down with a jerk on the sofa. 'If you'd been at the Moy that day, seen the state of him when they brought him in! I thought that they had killed him. I was sure that he was going to die. And I wasn't just afraid, I was filled with such anger, Alison! Looking down at him – that poor innocent, lying there like a corpse. My own Carson! They were wheeling him away to the theatre on a trolley, and I walked down the passage beside him. When they went in and shut those big doors in my face, I thought, I'll not see him again. I'll never see him again alive.'

Her voice faded. I watched her flicking imaginary dust from the lap of her skirt with a bridled energy both pathetic and disquieting. I could see she was far away, back again at the Moy with her shock and her fear, and I kneeled down and drew her against me, hoping that if I waited in silence, she would start to speak again.

'They gave me his glasses,' she said in the end. 'The frames weren't even broken, but one of the lenses was missing and the other was all crazed. I couldn't bear the sight of them,

116

they were horrible, really frightening, far worse than the look of poor Daddy. I don't know how to explain, but they simply drove me demented. I went wild – I broke them to pieces. I wrenched them apart at the hinges, and I smashed up the good frames, right there in the hospital corridor. I never told Carson about it. When he asked, I said no one had found them.'

She looked at me at last, and laughed a little hysterically. 'Well, I'm telling you now,' she said. 'It must be true that one's sins will out.'

I hugged her. 'I think you've been wonderful. Never mind about the old glasses! You have been amazingly brave and calm ever since. It was just the shock. It was probably the best way to work off a bit of your anger.'

Abruptly, she pulled herself free of me. 'There's too much about working off anger. That's one thing I learned that day, when I saw your father lying there – iniquity tramples on gentleness. It's all there in the Book, when the scales fall away.' She got up and stood clenching her hands in front of her body as if she were cold. 'There are some things that should not be pardoned. The wrath of the Lord is righteous. When I get on my knees, I don't pray for the strength to forgive His enemies. I pray for the courage to fight them. The time has come for vengeance.' She paused, and looked down at me where I sat at her feet, but her eyes were blank and she quoted mechanically in a monotone not at all like her own voice, 'and the Lord hath said, cursed be he that keepeth back his sword from blood.'

I stared up at her. I was accustomed to the rantings of the prophets; fundamentalist preachers continually harangue their faithful this way, and the language is very infectious. But I was deeply dismayed by the emptiness both in her voice and in her face, and I jumped up and grasped her shoulders. Whatever it was that possessed her, it was something wholly bad, and my instinct was to shake her, to wake her and make her withstand it; my mother was gone, and I wanted her back. Her small bones under my hands, narrow, light as a bird's, made this impulse subside, but the nervous strain of the evening was suddenly overpowering, and I vented it in a wail that came straight down the years from the nursery, a lost frantic 'Mammy! Mammy!', and was startled and shamed by my foolishness.

In fact, had I practised all day, no other appeal would have worked so well. The hint of madness that lay in the vacancy of her expression scuttled off at the good word, like a demon repulsed by an amulet, and her eyes filled with tears. For a moment I hoped she might cry with the healthy abandon needed to release some of her emotion but, even in face of my childishness, self-discipline and pride reasserted themselves, and she patted my hand, half in love, half in admonition.

'There, there – it's no use us fretting. No doubt we'll be shown the way to conduct ourselves if we seek for it.' Her eyes searched my face, sad and bewildered. 'My poor child! My poor little Alison! What makes you turn away from His infinite mercy and comfort? If you opened your ears you would hear Him.' And she added with unconscious pathos, 'I never cease to pray that you will be saved by His precious blood.'

She spoke simply, without the old undertones of reproach and indignation, and perversely I felt a surge of guilt. Resentment and bitterness were after all only a self-defence against my hurtful defection, a shield against sorrow and worry. She was genuinely afraid about the future of my lost soul; her most cherished hope was my salvation. She needed me, and I would fail her. I would never be able to share the faith that meant so much to her, and without it I was useless, not a joy and a consolation, but a further cause for despair.

So we stood there, in anguish and silence, each unable to bring to the other the support that we wanted to offer, much relieved to be able to smile and break the tension as we heard a shout from the stairhead above us, 'Come on to your bed now, Noreen! Do the spring-cleaning some other time! It's away after half eleven!'

'Listen to him!' my mother said fondly. 'You would think there was nothing to do in a house. Well, I'll set things to rights in the morning.' And she added, almost timidly, 'Maybe you would just check and see that the back door is locked, and the windows all shut?' Then she called out, 'I'll be up directly!' and turned quickly away with a light little kiss.

I watched her go. I knew that to ask me to make the house safe for the night was for her a degree of surrender, an admission of need and affection that had very little to do with the actual business of bolting a door, but I saw no way of responding. I had never known how to use such openings when she offered them. As I stood there a host of lost chances from the past returned to rebuke me. Gestures spurned, opportunities wasted. Their combined weight lay heavily on me as I made my way up to my room.

Sunday mornings have changed at Dunvarden, and it is not all my doing; my mother's rebirth drives a wedge through the house. Childhood Sundays were pleasant times, reassuring and monotonous, and particularly characterised by the feeling of being a family. We came down to a leisurely breakfast and savoured it companionably. In church we sat side by side, and went home drawn together more closely by the tedium of the sermon, or the fact that poor little Miss Davidson, deaf already and growing blind, had played all the hymn tunes out of order again. Lunch was large, and ritualised by much sharpening of the carving knife and a longer grace than usual, and it left us replete and languid. Weekday afternoons ended at five, when your mind turned to tea as the principal meal – but on Sundays they lasted for ever, and the unbroken hours had an air all their own, a dream aura of tranquil boredom, a constancy seeming to guarantee that no day would ever arrive when we four could not peacefully share them.

Nowadays, in blatant contrast, our disunion is worse on Sundays. Every difference between us is emphasised. My mother gets up betimes, and snatches a bite in the kitchen. The Pentecostal assembly meets comparatively early, well before the bell starts to chime for the Church of Ireland service at eleven, and besides she likes to make time to drive round by Jim's so that they can go on together, for the tin hut that serves as a meeting-house most inconveniently lies on the farther side of the valley.

My father does not come down until she is about to leave, and completes this silent protest by immediately getting out his car and following behind to O'Hagan's to fetch the papers. Sunday papers are not allowed to cross the threshold of Jimmy's house and, although there was once a time when my mother read them more avidly than anyone else, she now frowns on them, and of course upon those who buy them. My father strews them around without any concession to puritan views, and my mother retrieves them with sighs, and hides them away in a corner when she gets back from her devotions to an empty house.

Meanwhile, my father has departed all alone to morning service, often leaving his breakfast untouched on the stove. My mother greets this with surprise, though it must have happened a hundred times, and scrapes it away with displeasure, but she continues to cook it. I long ago realised that she courts his provoking rejection of food so that she can feel offended and take refuge in *that*. Any insult is easier to bear than the real pain she feels when she thinks of him, kneeling solitary and deserted in the family pew in the squat parish church in the centre of Killycreel where we used to worship together. This picture is harrowing, and the guilt that it carries insufferable: we are all acutely aware of it, and attempt self-justification in various different ways that combine to make Sundays a minefield where no subject is safe to handle, and a stray word can trigger calamity.

As I got out of bed the next day, and dressed for another Sunday – clean blouse, best skirt neatly pressed, and a pair of court shoes a lot smarter than the ones I would like to have chosen, but put on to please my mother – I reflected thankfully that however distressing the accident, it was bound to keep Father from matins. We would not have to dwell on his loneliness. He would still be tucked up in bed, or perhaps settled cosily close to the fire. He would know he was loved and cherished, and the empty pew and the sense of loss alike would be kept at bay by our obvious concern for him. As I bid my mother good morning, I could see the same thought had occurred to her.

'You'll look after Daddy,' she said, 'and make him eat up his breakfast?' She was cutting the rind from some bacon, with one eye on the clock. Beside her an enormous hymn book lay, with her gloves and her hat on top of it. Both of these looked starkly new, as though just unwrapped from their packaging, and they were the same shade of magenta as the blouse that she was wearing. It might still be necessary to give thanks to the Lord in an old Orange Hall (though the funds, praise be, were growing) but you were expected to dress yourself a little extravagantly, with a few cheerful splashes of colour to show that your heart was rejoicing and your secular life was prosperous. The matching accessory was almost a uniform up at the Hall: a lot of white in summer, with turquoise or pink as a second choice, and for winter electric blue, emerald, or a scatter of scarlet. No woman

121

attended bareheaded, and the virtual ban on cosmetics exploded riotously in a mêlée of net and dyed feathers. The scrubbed faces that could be seen, unadorned beneath this finery, seemed oblivious to any paradox. Despite his demands for austerity, it was plain for all to see that the Lord had made honourable exception for hats. . . . Though this licence did not cover newsprint, it encouraged me to say that I would slip down to O'Hagan's to collect the Sunday papers for Father to read with his breakfast.

Outside, a dour winter day had succeeded yesterday's brittle truce. A damp breeze blowing up from the sea carried with it the smell of the estuary at low tide, iodine and dredged mud flats, and the black oily silt of the harbour. The essence of Killycreel seemed to whirl irritably around me, through my hair and my clothes and my body, with a loveless but unflagging wish to possess.

I crossed the yard hurriedly, diving into my car like an animal that plunges into its burrow, and slammed the door shut on the predatory wind. But when I turned the key, there was no response from the engine, not even the sulky thumping I associate with flat batteries. I sat there stupidly, making all the same motions again and again in a futile determination to deny the plain fact that the motor was dead. A panic swept over me, as appalling as it was irrational. I felt someone had severed a lifeline, had removed my last link with the actual world. Nowhere else could offer me a release from the chill claustrophobia outside. All freedom and sanity was contained in the module around me. The very litter was precious: Robin's sweetpapers still in the ashtray, the air-ticket stubs that Ben always scatters behind him like footprints, the muddled evocative smell every car absorbs from its owners – in the suffocating dark of this narrow country, such things had acquired an unreasonable significance; they were proof of another existence.

I sat quite still in my car for a long time before I went back to the house. My mother was crossing the hall with a tray held aloft, and her hat skewered in place. I had forgotten the way that she carries a tray, shoulder-high, proud and stiff, like a very superior butler, and the look of her rattled me further. I had no wish to find her brave or touching beneath her ridiculous hat, worn for a ridiculous service in a church that was driving her out of her mind; but I did, and the pang made me angry. I snatched the tray rudely from her.

'For heaven's sake,' I said, 'I told you I'd bring up his breakfast! Can't you let me do anything for you? You'll be late getting down to Jimmy's.' I went firmly on up the stairs without looking behind, for I knew that her face, upturned on the landing below me, would make me feel worse, more disloyal myself, more resentful at her for the way she contrived to turn even stupidity into some obscure advantage. My haste and my irritation made the cutlery clash on the tray.

My father was looking much better. No cajolery seemed to be necessary to make him attend to his breakfast. He sat up purposefully in bed and began to eat with enthusiasm. I remembered my promise to Jimmy and my mother's unwilling appeal for my help. Now that we were alone I must talk to him; must reopen the delicate subject of Pat, and tell him what Jimmy had said; must persuade him to go for a holiday for which he had no inclination, and which he would interpret correctly as a perfect chance for his son to usurp his remaining authority. I had small stomach for the assignment. Cravenly, I sought for a respite.

'Shall I go for the papers?' I said. 'I'd have fetched them by now, but my car wouldn't start. I can't think how I'll manage tomorrow.'

My father looked up to answer me, but instead returned to his egg and listened with quizzical patience as I grumbled on, easing my conscience by making a fuss about nothing. I was due up in Antrim by ten for my rendezvous with the packers.

123

How was I supposed to get there? How could I collect my paintings? Billy Ritchie would not leave his bed until long past the hour when I must be away, and today he was shut for the sabbath. Call that a breakdown garage! No one who was right in the head would put up with it for a minute . . .

As I paused to regain my breath, my father said gently, 'Come on out of that! Young Billy's a fine mechanic. It's not *his* fault we're all of us moidered to death.' He patted the edge of the bed. 'Just sit easy a while, you'll be back on the road soon enough. I'll get Billy shifted. And tomorrow you'll take the Rover.' He pushed aside his tray. 'But this morning I'm going to go out for a spin.'

'You'll do nothing of the kind!' I could hear my voice, sharp with surprise and alarm, and I tried to moderate it, to sound resolute but reasonable. 'It's no day to go for a drive. You'll sit in by the fire, like a sensible man who's recovering from an accident, and who wants to get fit just as soon as he can.'

'Fit for what?' my father exclaimed. 'Fit to do as my family tells me?' An unwonted sarcasm lay at the back of the words, though he smiled as he spoke. 'You're your mother all over again when you put on that voice, and it's never worked yet!' He sighed. 'Be that as it may. Today I must go up to Patsy's, and I'd better get myself weaving.'

This was worse than I expected, but as I began to protest, he threw back the blankets and waved me aside. 'Now don't give me a load of the Jimmies! He's been at you,' he looked at me shrewdly, 'yes, I thought so. And no doubt he's said that I must be kept out of the Old Town? Right again? Well, don't bother your head to repeat the whole thing, for I've heard it before. Just you tell him his father said that he'll walk through the streets of the town of his birth, without fear, till his legs cease to bear him.'

I interrupted harshly, 'If Jim's right you may find that your legs won't carry you much farther. The Old Town's a virtual ghetto, we're not welcome there any longer. Jim's convinced that they all wish us dead, and the Houricans, most particularly, are suspected by the authorities.' I could not meet his eyes with conviction, but I told him what Jimmy had said – about Colm, about the fingerprints, about hornets' nests and traitors, about steering clear of trouble.

By this time he had got out of bed and was rummaging in his wardrobe. I knew he was not really listening. He unearthed a favourite garment, a great rug of a dressing-gown that had taken the last thirty years in its stride. Even now it suggested authority, soothed fevers, bad dreams dissipated. Its appearance in the night had put paid to the horrors, the spectres, the fears, to wee Aidan's smashed skull in the orchard, to the creak of the bogeyman coming upstairs. It had represented the light in a world that was blind, and it spoke of it still, though the threat was no longer illusion and the wearer no longer infallible.

'If you're sure you have finished,' he said, 'I had better get shaved. It's high time I was off. Why the height of foolhardiness would be to run into your mother when I'm disobeying instructions! Now that *would* be calamity for you.'

He glanced hopefully into my face, but something in my expression made him drop the brave effort at banter. He continued without any drollery, 'I'm as safe in the Old Town as I am sitting here by the fireside. In fact I'm probably safer. If there's to be vengeance wreaked on me in connection with Patsy's death, they'd not want me destroyed at a Nationalist wake, that's the wrong image altogether. It would sicken a lot of potential support and it wouldn't look well in the press. Jimmy knows that as well as I do. It's his own boys that he's afraid of. I dare say they've been reading the riot act, telling him to see Daddy behaves and exhibits some solidarity.' He peered moodily into the looking-glass. 'No wonder I frightened Ruthie. Did you ever see such a face? Every colour of the rainbow . . . No, I'm nobody's puppet, Alison. My nightwatchman's been killed at his post on my gates, and my duty's perfectly plain, even leaving all personal feelings aside – though dear knows they would drive me there anyway.'

He broke off. He still stood with his back to the room, but the mirror betrayed his dejection, his loneliness and his courage. The familiar dressing-gown, with its ravelling cords and tassels, no longer fitted him properly. It was too large for him, and too heavy.

'I'm coming with you,' I said. 'You're not fit to be out in the car on your own.'

He said vaguely, 'Very well. I'd be grateful for your company. Pat thought highly of you as a youngster. And of Jimmy too. God rest his soul.'

I picked up the breakfast tray, and left him alone with his memories. Jim would think me both weak and perfidious. My mother would feel that her efforts to overcome her pride and appeal for my help had been thrown in her face. But I knew that I had no option. There was nothing that anybody could possibly do or say that would change my father's decision on this sort of moral issue. Once his mind was made up, he was adamant. It would be to no avail to plead my mother's anxiety, or to underline Jimmy's censure; he was quite aware of their feelings, and dismissed them. What worried me was that he might be wrong, that he might well be faced with the fact that their charge was well founded.

I had tried not to dwell on this prospect myself, but it suddenly seemed all too likely. A vision of Nanny Magennis presented itself to me as I stood by the sink. Nanny brimful with guile. Nanny vitriolic and scheming. 'Poor little Mrs Magennis' – he had simply not seen that she was aquiver with malice and national pride. He had thought her devoted and servile. Was the concept of loyal Wee Patsy every bit as illusory?

My father insisted on going on foot up the last stretch of hill to the Houricans'. The Rover was too big and formal, he said, for one who came privately, as a friend rather than an employer. I had thought this to be a misjudgment. Pat himself might have seen the distinction, but honouring the dead was a duty observed in the Old Town with as much show as you could muster, and reflected the social standing of your family and friends. Lavish gestures were seen as a compliment, and restraint was not in order.

Yet as I walked beside him, I realised he was right. His presence transcended his bandages, his stick and his painful progress. The Rover would have been superfluous and, as we drew nearer the house, I saw that it might have been galling as well, for the usual exuberance was missing, the emotional safety valve seemed to be shut. The mourners who climbed up the hill, or passed us on the way down again, looked withdrawn and introspective and, though they greeted my father, they did so uncomfortably, and no one fell into step with us. Small groups discussing the tragedy grew silent as we approached them; their eyes darted furtively from one to another, and did not meet ours. We were clearly an embarrassment: the car would have offered the perfect excuse for our troubling presence to be interpreted as provocative. Within it we would have been symbols, the emobidiment of them ones, nosing round where they should not be, and pretending concern in an incident that demonstrably could not have happened had Ireland been left to the Irish ... But deep though these feelings ran, they could hardly be aggravated by the sight of Mr McMurtry, a well-liked and much respected member of the community, limping to the wake of his murdered friend on the arm of his only daughter. No anonymous

Protestant patronage here. Albeit reluctantly, many people were moved by the look of him. Dear help him, the poor auld crittur, only out of his bed at the hospital, and struggling up the hill to pay his respects! Sure, you'd hardly know that he wasn't one of your own ones! A right civil big man.

Once, these thoughts would have found immediate and fervid expression. Reminiscence and condolence would have been shared, hands would have been formally wrung, tears copiously shed. Mutual innocence, mutual sorrow and mutual anger would have been assumed between us. 'I'll tell ye – the boys that done this thing are never from Killycreel! You'd not get a soul here to harm Patsy, nor yourself either, Mr McMurtry. You'd not find two better liked men though you'd search the whole Province for them!' But today these exchanges were absent. Tongues were checked by the weight of uncertainty. From whatever source it came, the fear and intimidation of years had closed minds and soured responses. No one trusted a Protestant nowadays and the strong suspicion that Jim had destroyed his father's resistance to the wilder claims of bigotry, made the new scepticism stronger. Old McMurtry might climb the hill to Pat Hourican's wake, but what practical help was that in a town of trouble? What was happening down at McMurtry's yards? The old man had reared a son who would never employ a Catholic, that was plain as the ears on a donkey. Had the Provos attempted to kill him? It was certainly whispered by some that they wouldn't have scrupled to sacrifice Pat. On the other hand, it was said that the Boys were very angry, had no part in the whole bungled business, that it all was the work of the U.V.F., in which case, the blame for the death lay square on the heads of the Protestants. Either ways, what was there to say to one of the Others at times such as this?

Undeterred, my father trudged upwards. The cobbles were steep and uneven. He was weak and his bad eye was still almost closed. I was walking with my hand underneath his elbow to steady him, and I felt each rebuff run through him like a small electrical impulse, yet he met every shifty face, every half-hearted nod and mutter the forlorn little street had to offer him without any discernible sign of offence. He simply raised his hand in the local manner of greeting in response to each slight and evasion, and I marvelled at how much the gesture conveyed. It can mean almost anything, this half-wave, half-salute: a farewell, a good-day, the acknowledgement of an order, a how-do-ye-do between equals, or the gracious benison of a Brian Burns. In my father's case, it expressed courtesy and sorrow, and an assumption of kinship that retained its integrity in the face of all vicissitude. He had never been imposing, he was not cast in the heroic mould, but his probity lent him a grace that came very near to stateliness. It carried him forward with honour, and left momentary shame and confusion behind. For the first time in my life I realised I was more than contented – I was proud – to be his daughter. In the midst of this maze of intrigue and mistrust, I was privileged to be related to something as absolute as my father's palpable goodness. If my confidence in his discernment had died, a new belief in him had suddenly replaced it: I was confident of his values, of his strength to uphold them though others did not. The truth he affirmed today would survive all onslaught upon it.

A small gathering of men melted quickly away from the threshold of Pat's house as we drew nearer, and we reached it alone and in silence. The blinds on the windows were lowered, as became a house of mourning, but the rickety front door with the black crepe fastened upon it stood open to the weather as a sign that a wake was in progress. My father dropped my arm and went forward without knocking. Every head in the room turned towards us, and for a long sickening moment as our bodies blocked out the light and the crowded gloom pressed round us, time and place seemed to warp. The sharp features of the old woman facing my father were Nanny's. Soon someone would say 'Who would you be looking for, daughter dear?' and I would answer 'Colm', and a terrible loss would consume me. The blurred ovals round the fire were the faces of Paschal, of Patsy himself; the girls were Colm's siblings . . .

The wheel steadied and stopped in the present. Theresa, her eyes rimmed with red, but wild with what seemed to be triumph, was advancing upon my father. She ignored his speech of condolence.

'I tould them ye'd come,' she said, 'but they none of them paid any heed to me. "The lot of youse wrong," I says, "he's not one to let Daddy away to his grave without he bids good-bye to him." ' She turned round shrilly on her family. 'I tould ye! But all of ye held he'd not come near the house for a fortune!'

As she paused, there was whispering and pushing and a younger woman stepped forward. 'Away now, Mammy,' she said. 'That's no way to be talking to visitors!' She glanced up, with her arm round Theresa. 'She's not herself, Mr McMurtry. The shock's put her clean astray. Why, we all of us thought you were still at the Moy.'

'Mairead's right,' said another daughter. 'We'd heard you were still in the hospital. Lord, but that's a quare eye ye have on ye!' She tried gamely to rally the thunderstruck room. 'Did you ever see such a head? Isn't he the stout man to be out with it?'

A chorus of ayes rewarded her. Tut-tuttings of sympathy began to be heard from the fireside. Several of the company came forward and shook my father's hand. A few conventional phrases became gradually more possible –

'A terrible tragedy!'

'Niver was a wee fella to match him!'

130

'Sure it's hard to believe he's been taken . . .'

But there was no heart behind them; they were awkward, stilted things, clumsily designed to skirt round the fact that Patsy had been murdered. There was no accord in the fractured talk. The enormous harmony so essential to the spirit of a wake house seemed to be frozen, and the whole healing power of the ritual – the catharsis of feeling free to express all emotion acceptably, to cry out to be helped and supported, had apparently disappeared with it. There was something else in the air, something shadier, more divisive, altogether less pure than anger. A degrading insidious poison: fear.

Fear paralysed the old men who might have been sharing fond memories of Pat, gagged the youngsters who should have been cursing his untimely and brutal slaughter. Fear kept women stiff-lipped, dry-eyed, lest a loose tongue betray something dangerous. For who knew any more what was dangerous? You couldn't be sure what the rights of things were. Somone had heard it said that the Boys had killed Pat as a lesson to those who were tempted to work for the Protestants; someone else that the Boys would avenge him; and there were rumours besides (rumours based on a dozen different tales) that this house was not done with trouble, and that worse was to come.

Yet the coffin was here. Decency dictated respect for it. And respect meant the family closing their ranks. In the absence of any guide as to whether Pat died a traitor, or a martyr, or a victim, his relations must do the best they could to uphold self-esteem and pride and lay on a dignified wake for him, and receive all visitors graciously. But the cost on the nerves was frightful. The things that might not be said lay about you like so many hand grenades. How could you mourn your dead when you didn't dare say what you thought to a soul? And to make matters worse there was Mammy. In

131

her grief she had no time for terror. Look at what she had just said, and worse, what she might yet go on to say during this most exacting of visits. Better try to discredit her while there was time.

'Thon poor woman, her wits is away!'

'She's done in, but they say she can't get till her sleep.'

'It's some tablets she'll be needing. Colm said he'd go down to the doctor's. Where is he, anyways?'

'He'll be doing his turn sitting up with the Da. Come on through Mr McMurtry. He's a beautiful corpus. Looks just like himself.'

The stairs were behind the kitchen, and they led almost vertically upwards. My father had difficulty climbing them. As he paused to regain his breath, two very old women came out of the room, one sobbing, one audibly praying, and both of them embraced us, blessing us and pressing our hands as the Hourican family once would have done.

'May the Lord keep you, Mr McMurtry! And the daughter too – God bless ye, darling! Sure I mind ye since you were a ba.'

They bent closer, secretive, fearful. 'Mary Mother, have mercy on us! Poor Wee Pat took like that and him still in his prime! Isn't that the desperate thing?'

'Sure, there's none that would do that but monsters!'

They crossed themselves nervously, and blessed us with greater vigour. As they hobbled away, still weeping, I thought suddenly of Matron. This was just what she had said, in a different tone, as we sat in the Moy. Yet the old women's home and refuge was to Matron the monsters' breeding ground. That monsters were never bred in this house or that, but were born of the void of ignorance lying between them, was a concept beyond understanding, and the few far-seeing men who attempted to act upon it were considered soft-witted or treacherous. I glanced quickly away from my father. He was already condemned by both sides of the community and I loved and admired him for it, but it was not easy to watch him. I followed him with dread as he limped forward into the little front room that Patsy had shared with Theresa.

It was stuffy and very cluttered. There was not much space left for the mourners. The ceiling sloped down to waist height at the walls, and someone had pulled out the bed so that people could shuffle round it. The enormity of this death, of all death-by-violence, became substance here. A profanity. A defilement. To breathe was to know its pollution. A foreign, unnatural smell of hospitals vied with the heavy air, underlining the fear and the horror with its own connotations of physical pain. Although we had tried to prepare for the evil and waste we might find in this room, we both flinched in instinctive panic from their almost tangible presence. My father jerked back his head as though something unpleasant had brushed past his face, and I found I had thrown up my hand as if to ward off an assailant.

Embarrassed, I let it fall, and made myself look down at Patsy. He lay wax-white in his coffin. The County had done a remarkable job. His head, though bald as an egg, had been carefully painted over to conceal any trace of injury; his features impossibly neatly arranged. His hands, crossed on his breast, had been scrubbed to resemble a plaster cast. Otherwise it seemed to me that there was nothing left of him. Neck and wrists protruded grotesquely from the collar and cuffs of an empty shirt. Tiny though he had always been, innate toughness had given him substance; now he looked like a finger puppet. A doll. A ventriloquist's dummy. The sight of Patsy dead would somehow have been more bearable than this aseptic travesty, so absurdly, so shockingly unlike a corpse. It was a mockery. An extenuation of wickedness. I knew I should bow my head as my father had done beside me, yet the thought of doing so sickened me. I could not pray like my father, nor make the sign of the cross like the old women on the landing: I wished to place nothing between me and the madness responsible for this death. The pointless bigotry, the aggression that posed as religious belief, as patriotism and honour; the delusion of superstition; the screaming floundering dark of ignorance and stupidity, all seemed to be met together in the small hell of this bedroom. To pretend to stand here and pray was in some part to submit to them.

Instead, I looked round for Colm. I was ready to condemn him. I wanted to find a target for the undirected rage that was so much more disturbing than an anger convincingly focused. If Colm had murdered his father, then he would personify all the savagery that surrounded me, and though this might be appalling, it was less bleak an option than staring into the dark and irredeemable madness that afflicted a whole province – to avoid that, I needed a scapegoat.

Yet the actual sight of him did not bring the expected catharsis. Standing there by his father's body, he did not look like a villain. He looked oddly dignified. And I saw that his dignity stemmed from the fact that, alone among his family, he was neither afraid nor bewildered. He was keeping his vigil with pride and defiance, and an anger, now plainly directed towards us, that more than matched mine in intensity. Whatever he might have done, he was certainly not ashamed of it.

Two little girls stood beside him, torn between the awesome excitement of goggling at the dead and the even fresher experience of appraising these strange new mourners, one of whom looked more battered than Grandda himself. The Prods had been after him too, judging by the shape he'd been left in . . . They began to whisper together, but a young woman rose from her knees at the sound and hustled them away. Then she came back and stood beside Colm, moving half a step in front of him. Her desire to defend was so obvious that I took her at once for his wife, and the force of her protectiveness brought a glimmer of warmth to the bedroom. I looked at her almost with gratitude.

She had a sharp starveling face, high cheekbones, a wisp of a body. The cheap provocative dress and the gaudy splashes of make-up that she wore seemed to make a statement that had more to do with courage than with any jauntiness. She was in her war paint. If bravado alone were needed to keep Colm from putting his head in a noose, then she had abundant supply. And if not? I returned a bright insincere smile that just failed to conceal the tension – and if not, she was wild enough, cornered enough, to resort to anything that would help save him from his enemies. What would I do, I wondered, if a system that I had been reared to distrust was gunning after Ben? Would I look kindly on its ambassadors? Accept their assurance of friendship? Or detest them as double agents?

My father had finished his prayers, and now he moved round the bedside. Etiquette allowed him no option but to speak to Patsy's son and offer him his sympathy. But the look on Colm's face reduced all the traditional phrases we had used downstairs to absurdity. The poor tattered pretence that, whatever our roots, we must all be on one side against terrorist atrocity, disintegrated before it. Yet the truth that my father embodied had never flamed so high. It was not founded upon niceties, and the lack of them could not harm it. He said quietly, 'I'm deeply sorry.'

Colm did not answer him, except with a withering sniff of contempt, but the woman covered this hastily, 'Why, poor Colm here's half demented! He was with the Da yesterday, and we all of us thought he was over the worst.'

Her voice dropped confidentially, but her eyes strayed towards Theresa who was just coming into the bedroom, and I

135

saw this was no welcome sight to her. Had the rest of them no gumption? What the hell did they think they were up to, leaving her up here all alone, with Colm near fit for the Mental, and these two bloody Prods snooping round him? And now letting Theresa away on them. She would give them a lash with her tongue that they wouldn't forget in a hurry. But meanwhiles she had better keep going . . .

She fell back on a well-worn comfort line, 'Such a peaceful face he has on him. Why, God love him, you'd think he was sleeping!'

We looked back obediently at the horrific waxwork that was all that remained of her father-in-law, and she continued familiarly, 'You'll be feeling the loss of him too. Sure, the Mammy's never done telling us how highly you regarded him.'

Colm spoke. 'Well, he's paid for your "regard", if that's what it was,' he said, 'and I hope you're pleased with the price you've got.'

Theresa whipped round like a viper. 'Will you shut your trap, Colm Hourican? There's your Daddy lying dead, and two friends of his come to pay tribute. I niver heard the like of ye!' Her shriek was worthy of Nanny but, as though she believed us deaf to this trifling family dispute, she resumed her former manner and turned back pleasantly towards us.

'Colm's taking it bad,' she said. 'Sure, he saw the Da only five minutes before thon buggers got up to their mischief. He was down bringing him the piece box. If he hadn't come away . . .' she broke off and glared from the coffin to her son in exasperation, 'but the Daddy and him, that's the way that they were – niver quit carpin' on, night and day, one as obstinate as others. Anything would get them going!'

She looked up at my father for moral support, 'Sure, there's no respect left in the youngsters! Ye can't get any manners drummed intil them! I tell ye, that very day, when Colm got back and I asked him whether he had seen the

136

Daddy, I had to berate him for saying he'd spied a monkey in a zoo who looked a wee bit like him – "but he wouldn't open his cage, Ma, so I passed him his dinner through, and I left him peepin' between the bars". He's a rough mouth on him, our Colm! But he thought the world of Patsy, and with all respect to you – as you'll understand Mr McMurtry – he wanted him out of the timber yard. And the Daddy, he made a big fuss about how he owed a lot to you, and he had to mind the security. He'd not hear a word said against you, not from Colm nor anybody. "He's a fine man," that's what he'd say, "a fine man, and this town needs more like him." Sure, even when Colm abused him . . .'

'I never abused him,' said Colm. 'I just warned him that nowadays there's no time for that kind of soft talk, and one Prod's just the same as another. I told him there was a war on – that no Catholic in Killycreel could be seen sitting on the security gates of a Loyalist firm like McMurtry's without getting what he was looking for. But the auld eejit paid no heed – and where is he now? In his coffin.' He looked across at my father. 'And there's others that well could be joining him there.'

His wife interrupted him with a voice like a slap, 'Ach Colm! Are you out of your mind completely?' Her face hardened with desperation. 'Have you no respect for the dead?' She seized his shoulders and shook them. Why did nobody come to help her? If he wasn't made quit this blether, he would talk them all into the Maze. And the old woman was no better. The wee'ns left to beg for their dinners! Jesus, Mary! She edged her way round to the door and hollered for Mairead.

But surprisingly it was Theresa who provided the vital distraction. Stupefied by the horror and speed of events, the stark fact of Patsy's death until now had scarcely reached her. All the time she had been speaking she had sounded no more than indigant and vexed, but something that Colm had said had apparently cut through the fog of her shock. She was suddenly racked with sobbing, her face fixed in a glaze of astonishment. Harsh dry sounds tore through her chest and shook her as if they would wrench her apart.

For a second the sound transfixed us. We stood rigid, a room full of statues. Then my father's walking-stick fell, and the clatter it made brought us all back to life. He grasped Theresa's hands and chafed them gently between his own. I put my arm round her shoulders. Colm's wife hurried back from the doorway. Mairead, answering the call, appeared magically beside us, and we all soothed and murmured and patted, the true soul of a wake house restored to us. Here was grief, normal grief, its familiar demands for comfort were liberating. We had all forgotten Colm. This was no work for virile young men, though of course they had their uses. They could watch, carry coffins, greet visitors. They could run errands for the household –

'Where's Colm?' exclaimed Mairead, suddenly recalling this virtue. 'He said he'd go down to the doctor's. Why, there ye are! Send up auld Matthew to sit by the Da awhiles, and fetch us some sleeping tablets.' As he hesitated, she added, 'Are ye deaf, ye great galoot ye? Your poor Mammy crucified, and you standing there doing nothing! Away and get us some medicine!'

Colm went.

With much clucking and fussing, the rest of us urged Theresa past Pat's body and out of the bedroom, helped my father down the stairs, and settled them both in the kitchen. Theresa's sobs were subsiding, but the look of amazement remained in her eyes. Someone brought out a pot of tea and a plate of buns from the kitchen, and I was again transported to that other far-off occasion when, so unexpectedly, I had tapped a genuine kindliness in the heart of Patsy's household.

But this present accord was more brittle. The old stability, the old structure at its foundations, had become a quicksand of suspicion, and it trembled and shifted beneath us. Fear, at first insidiously, and now with a final triumphant attack, had destroyed any chance it might prosper.

I looked anxiously at my father. His face was grey with fatigue, and his hand shook as he held his teacup. He had done far too much already. No matter how strong his spirit, a return trip down the hill would be more than he could manage.

Trading on our shared role of caring, I pursued Mairead into the kitchen. 'My father's exhausted,' I said. 'I don't think that he's fit to get back to the car. We left it down by the convent.'

'Ach, dear help him, he shouldn't have took till his feet!'

'He was dead set on walking,' I said, 'and no doubt he intends to go back the same way – he's as obstinate as they make them. I'm not going to start arguing with him, I'll just slip through the yard, if I may, and go down to the convent and bring up the car.'

Mairead nodded. 'We'll mind him for you. He'll not know that you're gone till you're back again. Him and Mammy's talking away, and Fionuala – she'll keep them all going.'

A complicity flickered between us: women's work, women's cunning united us. We smiled ruefully at each other, acknowledging the way our old people conspired to ignore our advice – twice as hard to control as the childer! But we could not restrict our communion. Once our eyes met, it was more than plain that we shared the same anguish, the same hopelessness.

Mairead's glance slithered off in confusion. She could hold no such traffic with Protestants. She would sooner end up in the Maze than be sucked into fellowship with them. This was Jimmy McMurtry's sister, and if ever there was a Loyalist who deserved his place in hell, then young Jim was your man, no mistaking it. She felt shamed by her moment of weakness, and her face hardened into a cold hostile mask. What did *she* care about my father? She cared nothing except to be rid of him. Her own father was lying dead, murdered (if not in fact, then in spirit) by the brother and the son of these diabolical visitors.

She hauled the back door open. A chill wind flurried into the kitchen. The small yard was a whirlpool of rubbish and rain. She watched me pick my way through the junk and the bins and the puddles, but when I reached the road and turned back to wave goodbye to her, she made me no answering signal. She regretted our fleeting contact, and she wanted to tell me so.

The Old Town was at Mass. The cathedral bells in their high mock-Gothic steeple still vibrated and sang in the back of my brain, but in fact they had given way to lesser peals from the valley. The flat monotonous clanging from the granite tower of my father's church, and the distant more musical chime from the big chapel serving the New Town still competed across the river. Soon all Killycreel would be at worship. Every man, every woman and child would emerge with their loyalties reinforced, their prejudices strengthened and their different tribal entities a little more polarised.

I thought of my Mother and Jimmy, of Heather and Ruthie and Ian, sitting on their uncomfortable benches, or singing fortissimo to the strains of the portable organ till the tin hall reverberated with the savage primitive imagery that made the adrenalin flow:

> 'Oh, wash my soul in Jesus' blood,
> Jesus' blood, Jesus' blood!
> Wash my soul in Jesus' blood
> Till it is white as snow . . .'

thus prepared, listening to the sermon, thundered out in the usual mixture of the Biblical and the vernacular. 'Know you what the Master has said? "Where the truth is, the lie must be vanquished, trodden under foot by the righteous! Before Peace, there comes War! I am come to set man at variance with his father, and the daughter against her mother; and a man's most dangerous foes may be found among his own household." We can have no truck, brothers and sisters, with the so-called ecumenicals, who run in harness with Rome, and with Rome's bitter hatred of that Perfect Truth, the Truth of the Reformation! WHERE THE TRUTH IS, THE LIE MUST BE VANQUISHED! Though best friend become fiercest foe, Romish falsehood must be expunged utterly! For Truth's sake, we must fight with courage . . .'

Ruth and Ian, fresh clay for the potter's warped wheel. Jim already lost to reason. My poor mother tormented by conflict as the Reverend Stanley McClung prayed for Father's complete recovery, 'both of Body and of Spirit, for what avails bodily vigour if the Spirit is sick within?'

I could picture it now, as I hurried downhill past the houses whose owners were hearing an entirely different message. Tears of rage welled into my eyes, and my anger increased at my loss of control. My father did not cry, and he had to bear this torment daily.

I turned my face into the rain that my cheeks might have some good excuse to be wet, and saw the Catholic cathedral rising straight in my line of vision. Here the congregation would pray, with a sense of passionate outrage, for the soul of Patrick Hourican, latest victim of ancient injustice. It would fall to the clergy to see that this outrage survived the service, and they would not want for a leader. The Diocesan Bishop O'Brádaigh (who now spelled his name fancifully in the Celtic way, to the bafflement of his old father, Master O'Brady) was a patriot and a scholar. He spoke brilliantly,

141

deviously, a Machiavellian preacher. Word for word, he could not be faulted – not quite – by the Press or his Mother the Church, yet his fervent sympathy with the cause of his nation flowed out to his flock. He inspired. He consoled. He exhorted those who wearied of the struggle to remember their militant comrades, to get down on their knees and pray that they might endure persecution without giving way to violence. For violence, of course, was appalling. All Christ's children must strive to renounce it. What though they should be surrounded, taunted, tempted every day by its outward manifestations – guns, and tanks, and uniformed soldiers? They must rise above such provocation. Christ had chosen the path of peace, and had urged it upon his disciples, themselves suffering foreign oppression. And the path of peace had triumphed! So even in these dark days, we must urge those hot-headed enough to enrol in Oglaigh na hEireann to turn aside from violence. He must ask everyone to pray, not only for the spirit of their brother Patrick Hourican, but for those who had brutally murdered him . . .

Yes, Pat's wake would be well attended. Friends and neighbours, uplifted by national zeal, and elated by the way that their martydom and their subjection had been affirmed by their bishop, would feel a renewed sense of purpose. They were fighting a crusade, a national battle, a holy war. And not, as they sometimes suspected in their loneliest lowest moments, a shabby and vicious campaign, engineered by a handful of madmen, and sustained by its own ugly impetus. No! Whatever had happened to Patsy, he had certainly not died in vain. Irish unity, somehow, was nearer at hand . . .

I made myself walk more slowly. I had been almost running: not running because it was raining, but literally running away from the prospect of facing the Old Town's ill will when morning Mass was over. I was bankrupt of courage and staying power. What was it my father had said? He would walk through the streets of the town of his birth without fear till his legs ceased to bear him. Well, I was not like my father. I was lonely and afraid in this sour deserted thoroughfare that made me feel like an outcast, and I wanted to be gone from it. As I reached the convent square, the full force of the rising storm blew in my face, and I felt a perverse satisfaction, a twisted masochist's pleasure. Dirty weather. Dirty town. Dirty dealings among dirty people. I couldn't wait to leave them. We had nothing left for each other.

With my head bowed against the gale, and my spirits a little buoyed up by my spleen, I pressed on towards the Rover. It stood in the relative shelter afforded by the wall, on the half-moon of concrete the convent had spread at the feet of the Virgin Mary, who rose blue and white over the gateway. Behind her haloed head, the Old Town petered into extinction, a wasteland of boarded-up windows, closed-down shops and abandoned houses. McLaverty's Tyre Depot, Neeson Bros. Scrap Metal Merchants, and a couple of garage workshops squatted stubbornly on in the overgrown yards. A steep unsurfaced lane made a shortcut through this dereliction to the straggling start of the New Town, and its entrance lay just to the right of the car. As I fumbled for my key, Colm suddenly stepped from the turning.

In the second before he saw me, the innumerable meetings and trysts we had shared co-existed, assaulting me with an urgent confusing impact.

'I'll see ye by the dolmen.'

'Ach Colm, you'll get yourself foundered! This weather's setting in. Can you not get a coat outa Nanny?'

'Coats is only for namby-pambies.'

'Jimmy's gotta coat.'

'What did I tell ye? Coats is for the likes of him,' cycling fast, so I couldn't retaliate, 'sure he'd melt if he met with a raindrop!' Looking back, tongue stuck out, words belying the cheek, 'I'll wait on ye by the stone.'

Here we were again. Cars now, not raincoats.

'That's wicked weather, Colm! I'm just fetching the car for my father, I'll give you a lift up the hill.'

No reply, but he paused, staring at me. He could not civilly refuse me and that left him two possible choices, to get into the car with good grace, or express what he thought of my offer without any attempt at blandishment. As I watched the alternatives warring behind his impassive face, I already knew the outcome – circumspection was not in his nature, and although the car key was by now in my hand, I did not open the door, but stood with my palms on the bonnet, ready for the first round of the contest.

'I'd sooner walk it, Missus. You get your father home. I'll look after meself.'

His expression was blank, the snub coolly and steadily spoken, but old instincts, old tactics swirled round in my mind. If I pushed him a little more, he would say what he thought with a vengeance, and some truth would emerge in the telling. If I wanted that truth, I must press for it now.

'Don't give me such nonsense,' I said. 'What's the point of getting a drenching when we're going the same direction? You get in, and I'll run you up home right away.'

I gestured towards the door, but as I had expected, scorn twisted his face. His voice cracked with disgust and outrage.

'I'd as lief ride with the devil as in any car of yourn!'

This was even more scathing than I had forseen, but the freedom the words brought was heady. They delivered me from convention. They smashed the flimsy shell of caution and mendacity that had constrained me all morning. I felt suddenly drunk with liberty.

'And who do you ride with?' I said. 'With terrorists? With murderers? With the thugs who blew up the timber yards? Was it the devil you drove with when your father met his death?'

144

Colm spun round and slammed his fist down on the car. 'If ye say that again, I'll kill ye!'

In my heart I knew this was no serious threat – 'If ye tell Nanny on me, I'll kill ye!' Vintage Colm, an echo of childhood's disputes, it was that and nothing more. But I too was in desperation, and I seized the phrase, using it cruelly.

'You can save yourself the bother. Don't you know that half the town is saying the same thing about you? Or perhaps you find killing no trouble? If you want to get rid of the lot of us, go ahead! I'm waiting. Start now!'

We were shouting at each other, leaning over the Rover's bonnet, forgetful of our surroundings. Now the unspeakable had been said, the hysteria gripping us suddenly broke. On the instant we both were aware of how very conspicuous we must appear, hurling wild and slanderous insults beneath the bulk of the Convent. The empty, listening square, the invisible eyes behind windows – never in our long intimate childhood had we thus publicly exposed ourselves. Yet now with death in the air, we were recklessly courting attention, and we paused aghast, taut face confronting taut face. Pain and frenzy had stripped us both bare, reduced protocol to ashes.

Colm spoke through clenched teeth, 'Whisht ye, Alison! Do ye want the whole place alerted?'

And I hissed back, my anger still smouldering, 'Will you get yourself into the car? It's not me that's creating a spectacle! How'll it look if I drive off and leave you? And you running behind all the way up the hill?'

Saving face, he glanced sullenly down. 'I'll destroy the good car. Will ye look at me shoes? I'll tell ye, yon cut's in gutters.'

I knew this was capitulation. 'Well, never mind that now, a bit of mud never hurt anyone. Your mother needs her medicine, and my father's still pretty weakly. The house will be thronged after Mass, and I want to make sure he's away home by then.'

I sat down as though matters were settled, and, after a long anxious second, Colm got in and shut the door with a sharp slam of aggravation. Then he said with a terrible bitterness, 'He's a sight better off than my father. What the hell did he come up here for? Does he not think he's done enough damage?'

I said hotly, 'He's done no damage! He's just given your father a job at the works since the two of them were boys. And offered him his friendship.'

Colm gave a harsh snort of derision. 'Well, he's done for him now, no mistaking it. Da'd be fit and well today if he'd had his cards handed back to him and been given his marching orders. A bit more of that sort of friendship and we'll all be in our graves. Ask your brother if you don't believe me.'

'Now you mention it, Colm,' I said, 'you're the spit image of my brother! I'd hardly know which one was speaking. You've identical notions of friendship, though your standpoint's not the same.' I paused, trembling at the prospect of insulting a murdered parent, but I knew if I wanted the truth I must strike. Something heavy seemed lodged in my chest, and I had to breathe deep to get past it.

'He thinks no Catholic can be trusted. He says Father was mad to go putting a man with a son in the IRA in charge of the security, and the outcome was always inevitable – sabotage and betrayal, an inside job. He believes that Patsy knew that my father might die in the fire-bomb attack, and was not too concerned by his conscience; that he was ready and willing to open the gates to you.'

'And that then I went in and killed him?'

'Either you or whoever was with you. And there's others who hold that opinion.'

'Half the town, isn't that what you said? Including the authorities?'

'Yes.'

We did not look at each other. Our voices were neutral, quiet, matter-of-fact.

'They've got evidence,' I said. 'Enough evidence to lift you. They know you were down at the quay when the bomb went off at the timber yards.'

'Before it! I wasn't there when the bomb went off. If they've evidence that they claim proves that, then they've faked it.'

His extraordinary calm deserted him. 'Is there nothing they do wouldn't sicken ye? The dirty filthy bastards! I don't blame them for framing me, but me father was straight! He'd as soon have betrayed his position down at McMurtry's as took Ulster single-handed. He'd never have let me through, though I'd lain on the pavement outside thon gates and yowled to get in like a baby. The security was like religion to him.' He gripped hold of my arm in his anguish, 'You go and tell that to Jimmy! Tell his friends! Tell it to the authorities! That's the way he would want remembered. Politics didn't matter to him – I'd his heart nearly broke with my carryin' on, we could scarcely speak but we quarrelled.' He turned blindly away. 'Well, we'll quarrel no more.'

I made no move to answer this outburst. I could feel he was close to weeping. Tears had often overcome Colm, however furiously he had fought the humiliation. To weep now would shame him profoundly. To give him time to recover, I started the car clumsily, fiddling round with the choke and the handbrake.

'Thon's a heavy auld bus to be driving.'

'Yes,' I said, 'but my car's broken down up at home. It'll have to go into Billy's.' I backed up to the Virgin Mary, adding conversationally, 'I'm for Antrim in the morning, scrake of dawn, so I'd better get used to it,' but I left the engine idle. From the corner of my eye, I could see that he

147

looked better, that the crisis was temporarily over. I returned doggedly to the subject in hand.

'If you take some advice from me, you'll go into the station immediately and offer to make a full statement. You can say you'd not thought it important till now, but with your father dead, and you the last one to speak to him . . .' His face set at that, blank and mulish, and I felt my own temper rising.

'For God's sake, Colm,' I said, 'if you're innocent, go in and tell them. You must have some explanation.'

'Explanation for what exactly? Not even the RUC have started lifting people for bringing their father a piece-box.'

I said nothing, and after a moment he shrugged and went on grudgingly. 'There's nothing I done that concerns them. I went down and rang the bell, and he come to the gate as usual. I didn't ask him to open it – I tell ye, he never un-locked it for me. I'd the lorry parked on the bend, and I wanted home to Fionuala. I just pushed it between the rail-ings, and exchanged some remarks about him working late. That's the truth. But it won't suit *them*.'

'That's a daft attitude! All they want is the truth.'

'Not this time. What they want is a frame-up. Someone's made a quare balls of a warning attack – one man injured, another dead. And your upright Loyalist gangsters, they don't want the responsibility, they're not ones to get nailed for murder. If they could pin it on me, they'd be only too delighted. They've got some old scores to settle. Do you re-member Joe Baker?' For the first time, he almost smiled. 'Ye blattered him with your schoolbag! He's not changed much that I can see, and he's on this investigation. He's become very great with your brother.'

I ignored this inviting diversion. 'What was it your father said about working so late?'

I could see that this was a very unpopular question.

'Ach, nothin'.'

148

'Come on now, Colm.'

'Well you're asking for it,' he said, 'but I tell ye, you're not going to like it. He was meant to come home that evening – that's why he hadn't his piece-box. But he said Harry Colley took ill, and left word that he couldn't come in for his shift. So Da stayed and sent up for his supper. He remarked that your father was still at the yard – he never quit harpin' on him – and he said he was waitin' on visitors. I asked who, but he come over secretive. Important ones, he said; he'd a message that they were expected.'

'From whom?'

'I didn't ask him. But "important" meant some of your ones.'

'But wait a minute,' I said, 'my father was actually leaving. He was just by his car when it happened. He wasn't expecting visitors.'

'Just so.'

'Then in that case,' I said, 'someone Patsy knew and trusted had pretended an appointment . . . had gone through all the proper formalities . . .'

'Exactly.'

As he replied, he regarded me with the patient regret of a nurse dealing with a halfwit, and I cried with exasperation, 'Then for Christ's sake, man! Go down and tell it to them at the barracks!'

'Do you think my father'll rise to corroborate my statement? Some of them's in this up to their oxters, and the rest would niver believe me.'

'Well, I believe you!' I cried.

'Aye, but we was like brother and sister.' He spoke simply without any sentiment, in pragmatic explanation. 'Ye'd always know if I lied.'

I tried once more. 'I beg you Colm. It's your duty to everybody. To yourself. Above all, to your father. Despite everything you say, there are fair laws and decent policemen,

149

incorruptible judges and magistrates. The judiciary in this country is not run by the likes of Jim.'

Colm slapped his hand down on the dashboard. 'I don't recognise this judiciary! Nor this "country". My country is Ireland.'

He drew back, and I knew that for him an iron curtain had dropped between us. I remembered him in the square underneath the hospital windows, spitting at the kneeling marksmen, and the way he had rallied the grovelling boys. Now his face wore the look I'd glimpsed then, and it could have been hewn out of marble for all the warmth there was left in it. A fanatical face, closed to contact. A lost face. A dead face, like Patsy's. In an inadvertent recoil from it, I buried my head in my hands.

I suppose I sat there for some minutes. I was not aware of their passing. With my eyes shut time seemed unimportant. Voices clamoured and raged in my head.

'Are you off your bap completely? There's a war on in this province.'

'We don't want any dirty old Catholics here!'

'Fucking British gits, go home!'

'Pardon me, if you please. I'm an Ulsterman. Ireland is a foreign country.'

'I don't recognise this judiciary.'

'The fearful menace of Rome must be seen as the ultimate enemy.'

'Mary Mother, have mercy on us!'

'The time has come for vengeance. What's this country coming to that we meet and treat with the devil?'

I tried to think of my father. 'We are all responsible, Noreen. We rear our children like heathens to despise their fellow men; we spawn preachers and politicians who have never learned humility . . .' It was hopeless, but I felt comforted.

I was visited again by a rare dry beautiful summer: Nanny's bony old cow short of grazing, smuggled daily to poach on the neighbour's land with her white-faced calf at her heels, and Colm and I in attendance, the lie ready – 'She broke out, Mister. We was trying to get her back outa yer field.' Keeping watch in the shade of a tree, chewing grass, listening to the Lambeg drums, insistent and threatening as tom-toms.

'Ach, I'm sick of your ones and their racket.'

'Sure, they'll quit once the Twelfth is by. They're just getting in thrim for the marchin'.'

'Them Prod songs leave me fit till be tied. All the words is about ownin' Ulster, and skelpin' the hell outa Catholics.'

'Well, your ones has songs too – I just hark to the tunes. The auld words, there's no meaning till them!'

'There is so! There is when you're older.'

'Then I'm never going to sing!'

'When you're grown up, there's nothin' else for it.'

I felt a small flicker of pride. At least no one could say that I'd broken my pledge.

I said, 'I never did sing them.'

'Sing what?'

I opened my eyes. 'Oh, those Orangemen's songs that you said I would sing.'

Colm seemed to feel no surprise at the total inconsequence of this remark, and I saw that he now looked quite normal.

'I heard you'd married a Catholic.'

'An English one,' I said. 'but we didn't have long together.' I realised that the car was still running, and I put on the windscreen wipers and set off across the square.

'Aye, I heard that too. I'm sorry.'

'I've a boy who's himself all over.'

'Ah, thank God! Fionuala and me, we've just the two wee lassies.'

151

We drew up. The hill flowed like a river. Colm opened his door.

'Thon rain's chronic! Thank you kindly for the ride.'

'It's a pleasure.'

We dashed through the downpour and jumped over the foaming gutter, but he stood at the door like a sentry at arms until I had passed safely inside.

My father and I did not talk very much as we drove back to Dunvarden, and what we did say was trivial: did you ever see such rain, and yesterday like the Spring itself? We hoped Mother had remembered to bring an umbrella with her, or at least borrowed one from Jim – her good hat would get wrecked . . .

We exchanged a wan smile as we saw that her car was still missing. We each knew that the other had ardently prayed that she would linger at Jim's hoping for a lull in the weather, so that we might slip in undetected without need to give instant account of ourselves. Later on we would have to confess that we had been up at the Houricans', but just now we both craved an adjournment, a breathing space for recovery. We felt eroded, drained by the trauma of the morning. We did not wish to discuss it. Not yet. Not even between ourselves. We needed a little time to absorb and assimilate what we had seen, to diffuse the emotional impact and allow the shock waves to settle. It was out of the question to tell a direct lie to my mother, but postponed revelation seemed different. In the absence of awkward enquiries, awkward answers, perhaps, might be shelved?

We did not voice this thought to each other as we hurried into the hallway – that would somehow have made it more dubious. My father simply said he would go back to bed for a bit of a rest, and perhaps come down in the evening, and I picked up the damp coats and gutter-soaked shoes that we had left in the porch and shut them away in the boiler-room. Yet I feared subterfuge was useless. Mother was not blind, and it did not require a very discerning eye to reveal that my father had spent all his strength, or to lay bare my own collusion, it just needed one open, receptive glance. I could picture the scene vividly, and I quailed in anticipation.

As it turned out, I need not have worried. I had overlooked the influence that the Reverend McClung wielded over his congregation, how he closed eyes and paralysed senses. My mother returned from her service resolutely determined to see nothing that would rock her confidence; she had sought, and had found, shreds of comfort. Her husband had faltered upon the straight road, but the good Lord had seen fit that he should be taught a redeeming lesson. Now her hopes and her prayers would be answered. He would see how misplaced was his tolerance, how the perfect truth always must be both proclaimed and defended with vigour. No more countenancing idolaters. No more sanctioning edicts from Rome by championing those who obeyed them. No more employing Catholics. Above all, now that God had rebuked and restored, no more friction in the home. Even Alison – hadn't the Reverend been speaking to her of Alison, leaning out of the pulpit and holding her gaze with his powerful hypnotic stare, and reminding her that His merciful love would never deny salvation? If the lost lamb turned back to the beckoning fold it would always be welcomed in, no matter how smirched, how bedraggled. 'For provision is made most plenteously': that had been the text of the sermon. The lost lamb welcomed in. Her lost lamb. Prayer would bring it home out of the cold. Prayer and faith. She must trust in His mercy.

This fresh hope was in some ways more taxing to bear, and more pathetic to see, than the wrath I had been expecting. The self-righteousness maddened me, and the sad, stubborn courage was poignant. And yet as the hours went by, its sheer

153

positive force built a fortress for us, made a place where warm normal things flourished. As we acted the old happy Sundays, like a play within a play, we fell gradually under the spell that we wove. All that murder and mayhem and rain – the grim props of the main production – faded from the front of the stage, seemed less real than our cosy reprise of the past. Employing great tact and care, we built upon this illusion. The castle that rose in the air seemed more solid and sure if we stayed in one room, outside influence threatened its substance, and we catered to this by unspoken consent. We ate our lunch from trays, one on either side of my father's bed, and we did not discuss the morning. We ignored the distressing events of last night. I did not telephone Ben, as I'd promised to do when I last spoke to him. We thrust the present away and took refuge in reminiscence. We relived old holidays, recalled dead pets and vanished possessions, recollected past excursions, laughed together at fabled disasters.

'Will you ever forget the day Jimmy scattered the stalls in the market?'

'Wasn't that the old bull-nosed Morris?'

'Sure, he didn't know the width of it. He was learning to drive anyway, I don't think he'd been at it for more than a week.'

'Such a ruction! Old Hugh McAnulty – do you mind the look of him, Alison? And Old Mrs Whatshername? That kept the fish stall on the corner?'

'Mrs Boyle!'

'That's her! She went wild, slapped poor Jim round the ears with a fillet of plaice.'

'A fortune we had to pay. All those pears and bananas and herrings and cod.'

'Still, it taught young Jimmy a lesson. A right steady and sensible driver he made.'

'Oh, Carson,' my mother said, 'that reminds me, Jim asked

for the Rover tonight. They need the seats from the Hall for the children's Christmas party. There's a hitch on Dickie's car, but he's booked to preach down in Dungannon at six, and there's no one can pull the trailer. Jimmy said he'd help out if it's all right by you.'

My father laughed. 'There you are! We'd be lost without the old Rover. Hitch or no, there's a queue to use her. I should advertise as a removals man! McMurtry's shifts everything. Works of art to church pews!' He looked pleased nonetheless. 'Jim can have her tonight if he wants her, but we'll need her back for Alison. Did she tell you her fancy new car has got to go in to Billy's?'

'You don't say!' but my mother spoke absently, her attention still fixed on my father, and I did not pursue the subject. Instead, as she turned to me, we exchanged a brief grand-that-he's-joking grimace. Satisfaction flowed warmly between us. More proud battlements rose on our castle. By the time Jim appeared for tea, it towered sturdy and tall to receive him. After all, he was part of its fabric: a conventional Sunday evening, Jimmy bowling home cheerfully – from the rugger-pitch scrum, from the Boys' Brigade band, from an exercise with the Cadet Force. Here's our Jim coming now! Make the lad a fresh pot!

My father had got up again by the time he arrived, and the fire had been lit.

'I can tell you, that's some night!' he said, as he thawed his big hands. 'If it keeps up like this, it'll set the house back a fortnight. Let those builders get started on inside work, and I'm done for! Once they go, I'll not see them this side of Christmas.'

'It's no time of the year to be roofing.'

'They're behind schedule, that's the trouble.'

My mother looked up hopefully, 'Heather says you'll be in by Easter.'

Jimmy chuckled. 'Is that what she's saying? Dear, dear, the impatience of women! In by Easter! And why not by Christmas forsooth? She could sit up here in the snow with a tarpaulin over the rafters!'

'Ah now Jim! She's just feeling unsettled.'

'Heather feeling unsettled?' cried Jim. 'Who's been unsettled, I'd like to know? Who's been nagged into all this flitting? Poor old James! But so long as he's signing the cheques, no one bothers to think about *him*!'

He winked broadly at my father. Posing as two hen-pecked husbands was a standard game between them, only played because everyone knew they had dominance over their households, and I usually found it annoying. But tonight I was glad to find Jim on top form. He would make a better neighbour if he felt the decision to move was his own. Had Heather been bullying him, he would never have acted the browbeaten spouse.

I wondered what new factor had entered the question of moving. Though his house now stood in a maelstrom, the noise did not worry him, and the ugliness of his surroundings hardly entered his awareness. He was fond of his home and accustomed to it: all change was at odds with his nature, and extravagance too was anathema; to spend money properly meant to plough it back into the business. He had been exceedingly stubborn, and for years he had stonewalled all Heather's complaints – restlessness was a woman's whim, and unnecessary spending a female defect. When I heard he had given in, I had feared the surrender would rankle for life and that everybody would suffer; now it seemed that his choice had been willingly made. The relief that this brought to me left reality further behind by the hour.

When the time came for Jimmy to go, I went with him to look for the keys of the car which were still in my overcoat pocket, and to see him out into the darkness. Against the

black of the night, the porch windows threw back our reflec-
tions: three large brothers, tall and stocky; three small sisters,
short and slight, raindrops blurring their features and spot-
ting their clothes. Seeing them I felt suddenly lonely, loth to
see the small women deserted. For the first time in my life I
looked out of the door at Dunvarden and found its seclusion
desolate, the absence of lights melancholy, the unfrequented
road and the empty moor forsaken. I felt heartily glad Jim
was moving. His unsightly new bungalow and the scar that
it made on the landscape were a small price to pay for his
presence. When my parents looked out of their windows on
a night like this, his lights would transform the lonely prospect.

As though reading my thoughts, he said, 'I'll be glad to be
closer to them. They're not getting any younger. And life's
not getting easier, either.' He shrugged and pulled a wry face.
'They need someone to keep an eye on them, and it's ten
miles round trip now, from our place. Once we're in, it'll be
a lot handier.'

I looked at him gratefully: the good son, the reliable
brother. By comparison, I was worthless. In the dazzling
glow of those make-believe hours, it was difficult to see what
was wrong with this equation. Who had always looked after
my parents? Who was here when they needed comfort? Who
was now moving home selflessly, to protect and cherish them
further? Not their daughter. Not I, but Jimmy. For a moment the rest did not matter.

'Thank God you're here,' I said. 'I don't know what they'd
do without you.'

It was years since I'd spoken so warmly, years since I had
felt such obligation; and once the words were said, his surprise and his pleasure both fuelled my guilt. I felt I had been
niggardly, thankless. In making it plain to him that I knew
he had offered no sacrifice by staying at home in Ulster, but

had chosen the life he wanted, I had left myself no room to acknowledge his many real virtues. This visit was an example; even had he not needed the Rover, he would have come up today to bolster my father's spirits. 'I thought I'd just drop by' – that was always his phrase, though we all knew quite well he was not within dropping-by distance. Most especially not on an evening like this. I stared out at the scudding rain. Well, at least I could save him another round trip.

'That night's getting no better,' I said. 'You don't need to come traipsing back here with the car.'

'I thought Pop said you wanted to use her?'

'I can pick her up,' I said. 'I'll take your car down in the morning and go on from there in the Rover. But you'll understand if I don't come in? I'll just swap the cars round and away. I want to make good time to Antrim.'

'Are you sure? That would suit me well, but I don't want to put you to trouble.'

'Ach, don't be silly, Jim. I'll be passing your door.'

We exchanged keys and smiles. Jimmy turned up his overcoat collar and glanced down at his watch. 'Would you look at the time? They'll be waiting up at the hall. Are you still going back Tuesday evening?'

'Yes, so long as my car's fixed by then. I'm booked on the Belfast ferry.'

'I'll put the boot behind Billy, I can give him a ring from the office. And I'll drop by before you go, maybe Tuesday before you set out for the boat. Well . . .' he paused uncertainly, and I realised that he too had valued our truce, and was now reluctant to leave me. When he 'dropped by' on Tuesday evening he would certainly want to know if I had spoken to Father, and the subject would tear us asunder. Even now, in his heart, he was conscious of this.

'Well then, mind how you go! The Rover'll be round at the back of the house.'

'That's fine.'

'And I'll see you Tuesday.'

'Jim?'

He turned back immediately, but I suddenly knew I must not tempt my fate. This calm evening was only an echo, a mirror image of childhood. One serious word from me would shatter the resurrection like a stone hurled into a looking glass.

'Oh, nothing. You're going to be late as it is. See you Tuesday.'

'Right you be.' He put his hand out to the door knob, 'I was thinking . . .'

'Yes?'

'Ah, no matter. We'll get time to talk Tuesday evening. They'll be wondering what's keeping me.'

'Well, so long then. Take care.'

I remained in the porch while the arc of Jim's lights swept the gravel and disappeared round the laurels. For the second time that day, I had met with the ghost of a brother, and had watched him vanish before me. I had thought that such torment was over and done, yet here it was back again, an old bereavement restored to life, apparently undiminished. I had been unequipped to endure it anew, and was shocked by my own distress.

The storm blew itself out abruptly in the early hours of the morning, and the sudden stillness woke me. The big south-westerly bow of my window had caught the full force of the gale, and I had tailored my dreaming to the noise and the vibration; the fantasies still in my head were as crazy and wild as the weather itself. But now that the storm was dead, I was unprepared for the silence and I lay awake for a long time, cramped and tense, my mind miserably active. When I feel asleep at last, it was into that heavy drugged slumber that sometimes comes before morning and is as unrefreshing as sickness. The sound of the telephone bell reached me dimly through layers of unconsciousness. As I stumbled out of bed, my first thoughts were entirely selfish. It was cold. My head was throbbing. How could anyone phone us so early? Six o'clock! Had my father been well, I wouldn't have bothered to answer, but I did not want him wakened, or my mother frightened either. I was halfway down the stairs when the thought of my mother's fear kindled my own. What if something had happened to Ben? to Robin? to Heather and Jimmy? I ran across the hall and snatched up the receiver.

'Hello?' My mouth was dry, and I still felt unpleasantly fuddled.

There was no immediate reply, just a distant whirring and clicking. My anxiety changed to annoyance. This was just an untimely mistake or a hoax, and whoever was on the line was about to hang up without speaking. I said crossly, 'This is Dunvarden. What number are you calling?'

'Who's it speakin'?'

Slightly surprised, and increasingly impatient, I said brusquely, 'Alison Lacey. I should think you've got a wrong number.'

'Alison?' An uneven breath that was almost a gasp jerked me fully awake. 'Jeez, I thought I'd maybe missed ye. It's Colm.'

The words were completely distinct, yet I tried to deny my own hearing. Such a call was against all convention. Colm never telephoned. I had got it all wrong. It was somebody else.

'Are you still for Antrim this morning?'

Cold reality gripped like a spasm of pain. This was Colm without a doubt. But his manner was wrong, and this question of his, ostensibly so simple, was as false as the nonchalant tone of his voice. *Ye'd always know if I lied.*

I said carefully, 'What's the matter? Are you after a lift or something?'

There was a moment's silence. I wondered, was he on the run? I saw myself at a roadblock, Colm locked in the boot of the Rover, the broad uniformed chest at my window . . .

'Are ye still going to take the big car?'

'Yes,' I said. I too seemed to be fighting for air. 'It's down at Jim's at the minute, but I'm picking it up on my way through the town . . .'

He interrupted me. 'Don't you touch it!' he cried. 'Do ye hear what I say? Don't go anywhere near yon Rover!'

For a second the words held no meaning at all, then they penetrated my brain with the clear cutting edge of a laser. In the dislocation that followed, I was conscious of heightened perceptions, of the chill from the flags on the floor, of the way the light fell through the mullioned glass shade, of my breath misting the receiver, of the terror that came to me over the wire. I saw the man, the boy, the child I had known merge and separate with a strange surreal clarity. I remembered the night Nanny nearly died. I experienced total recall of the fear that had kept me at home in my bed.

'Alison? Alison! Are ye there? Keep away from the Rover – I'm telling ye straight!'

A killer, like all the rest? Or a man who was risking his life for a friend? Or both?

'I hear you,' I said. 'Thank you very much for the message.'

The telephone went dead. I looked up and saw my father. He was standing quite still, on the bend of the stairs.

'You've had bad news,' he said. 'It's all over your face.'

'Just a bit of advice. But we've got to get hold of Jimmy. And inform the police.'

'Aye, I thought so.'

He spoke quietly, and yet his words reached a new layer of apprehension. I felt something stir under my panic, the first twinge of a terrible quandary. I wondered how long he'd

161

been there, and how much he had heard, but we both held our peace.

He came slowly down into the hall and put his arm round my shoulders as I dialled my brother's number, and we pressed close together for comfort until Jimmy answered the call.

The next hour was interminable. We dressed and sat in the kitchen. We did not feel like eating, but my mother made some tea and tried to induce us to breakfast.

'At least get some toast into you, Carson! Why, your clothes are hanging off you!'

My father waved it away, 'I'm not hungry, Noreen. Have some yourself?'

But she did not want it either. All her thoughts were with Jim and the boobytrapped car.

'What on earth are they doing?' she said. 'It's ages since we rang them. I've a good mind to go down to Jimmy's. They've no right to expect us to sit here all day. They said they'd telephone . . .'

'And they will,' interrupted my father. 'They'll phone when they've something to tell us. You know they're great boys, and they'll stick by their word. If they want us sat here, we'll stay. It's far better for us to keep out of their road, they've enough on their hands already.'

'But Carson! Jim and the children!'

'They'll have got them out long ago. And they'll let us know soon. Why, it's early days yet.'

We all turned to the clock on the dresser. It was only a quarter past seven. Surely that could not be so? We glanced covertly at our watches, and then back again at each other. Yes. Only a quarter past seven.

'It takes time,' my father said. 'They'll have had to go round there and look at the car, and decide what to do about it.'

162

'I don't care what they do!' cried my mother. 'All I want is to see our Jim.' Her voice shook. 'If we'd not had that warning . . .'

'If we'd not had that warning,' I said, 'then I'd have been blown to pieces – not Jim.'

My own words made me feel rather sick. I held on to the edge of my chair with both hands and looked at my mother. She was under enormous stress, and of course she was worried to death about Jim. All my better self urged me to silence. We must go on behaving well, being mutually supportive, keeping calm, no explosions of feeling. After all, if my mother had not taken in what a narrow escape I had had, it was nothing but a good thing. I must pull myself together. In an effort to check my expression of hurt, I deliberately thought about Robin, but for once this solace failed. My own fragmented body became doubly obscene and appalling, and my mother's indifference more heartless. To my surprise and distress, I discovered my voice had a life of its own.

'It would be nice,' it said, 'if you showed some relief that your daughter's alive. I know that compared to Jim, I don't matter at all – still, in view of the fact that he's not in any danger, and his bigotry's nearly killed me –

'Hold on there!' my father cried, but my words tumbled out, quite beyond my control.

'Yes, it did – this was a reprisal! If I'd died instead of Jim, they'd have called me a Loyalist martyr!' I scraped my chair back from the table and stood up. I was shaking with anger. 'I won't be thought of that way! I'm no Unionist, and I belong to no church! I refuse to be part of this madness!'

My father shook his head wearily. 'But you are part of it,' he said, 'and you've got to accept it if you're to survive.' He rose too, and leaned over the table as though trying to make closer contact. 'Whatever you do or say, you're the Protestant child of a Protestant home – that's the way you'll be

163

judged in this country, never mind that for you it's irrelevant as the colour of your hair! You saw that plain enough, up at Patsy's.'

I suppose I stared at him blankly, for he brought out his next words slowly and with unaccustomed emphasis. 'What I'm trying to tell you,' he said, 'is that slighting your own is a dangerous thing, and it's not just yourself that will suffer. You'll bring trouble to everyone crossing your path. Look at me!' He threw up his hands. 'What's the outcome of my endeavours? A man has been sent to his death, and my own children are in peril.'

As he paused, Colm's voice came back to me, 'a bit more of that sort of friendship, and we'll all be in our graves'. And now where had his own friendship led him? 'Don't go anywhere near yon Rover!' We'd all seen what was done to informers.

'Don't mistake me,' my father said, 'I'm not seeking to change your opinions, but it's no time for misconceptions. It's a clear head that you're needing. If you carry on down this road, you must do so with your eyes open,' he glanced across at my mother, 'and be ready to sacrifice more than yourself.'

My mother bent forward abruptly. All the time he had been speaking she had sat there motionless, with her elbows on the table and her face half sunk in her hands, as though trying to distance herself from the scene. Now she laced her fingers together and the knobs of her knuckles showed white through the skin.

'I don't believe it,' she said. 'I just don't believe what I'm hearing! I thought I knew you, Carson, and now I hear you say that you'd sacrifice your own children for the sake of some hopeless ideal – that for years you have knowingly put us at risk!'

She flinched away from the hand that my father put out

towards her. 'No, please don't anyone touch me! I can't take much more at the minute. It's been hard enough living with you when I thought you were simply too decent a man to acknowledge the evil around you. But I've never doubted you'd put us first. Not it seems you care less for your son . . .'

She broke off as we all heard the sound of a car. We spun round and stared at the window, though the sky was still dark and the curtains were shut. No one spoke. Tyres crunched to a standstill and doors banged. Just outside the glass, we could hear the engine still running.

The expected rap on the door was polite and restrained, and immediately eased the suspense that held us frozen. 'That will be the police,' said my father, but as he went into the hall, he turned out the lights in the kitchen. 'Much better sure than sorry! Just stay there in the dark a wee moment.'

We heard the bolts being drawn and an outbreak of cheerful greeting, and I hastily snapped down the light switch.

'Good morning there, Mr McMurtry, sir!'

'Good morning to you, Hugh. How's things down in the town?'

'Not so bad, not so bad. They'll get worse before they get better.'

'Jim's not with you?'

'He's down at the barracks, with the wife and the wee'ns. Right as rain! Good morning, Mrs McMurtry! I was just saying to your husband that the family's all in fine order.'

They came in respectfully, a little behind my father. Both of them were known to me; Sergeant Gormley, whose brother worked down at the yards, and a young constable called McCluskey, son of one of the stewards at the Yacht Club. They stood there bulkily, somehow out of scale with the kitchen. Their flak jackets made them look bigger, their hats added an inch or two more to their height. Both were armed. Sergeant Gormley's revolver was a standard sight to see, being simply part of his uniform, but the constable carried a Sterling.

I looked across at my mother. She was pouring out cups of tea, and I saw none of this jarred upon her at all. Sub-machine-guns were part of the landscape, and if one appeared at breakfast (once you'd checked subconsciously, to make sure it was carried by one of your own) it was not worthy of your attention. That was life, nowadays.

'Sugar, Sergeant?'

'Thank you, Missus. Two for me.'

'Well now boys, what's the form? You're not here for your health.'

Sergeant Gormley smiled back at my father, and the constable slotted one thumb, large and blunt, through the shoulder-strap of his Sterling.

'Right enough! Well, the Super's arrived on the job, and he's takin' it very serious. He's calling in the Army. Built-up area. Centre of town. There'll be some quare commotion, I'm telling ye that!' He looked down, suddenly embarrassed. 'Anyways, we've been sent up to fetch you. And your daughter too, sir, if you please, since it's her took the call with the warning,' he glanced at me curiously, 'and the Super would like a wee chat with her.'

'Why, of course!' exclaimed my father, and my mother said anxiously, 'But you'll take me down too? I don't want to stay here.'

'Ach, indeed we will, Mrs McMurtry! Then youse'll all be together.' His tone, ringing with bonhomie now the awkward moment was over, made the prospect sound almost festive. We all trouped out good-humouredly, and squeezed into the grey, armoured Land Rover that waited to receive us. We spoke lightly of other matters as we drove down to Killycreel.

The RUC station behind the canal is known as the New Barracks. The original station was under the hill, at the foot of the Old Town, and had long been seen as a death-trap. Pride alone had kept it going through the long years of home-made bombs, snipers' bullets, hurled stones and armed ambush. When at last it was razed to the ground by a fire at the end of the seventies, its destruction was secretly welcomed. By some miracle there were no casualties. An untenable outpost was gone, and no face need be lost by rebuilding it in a more strategic position. The New Barracks went up with alacrity at the Protestant end of the town, in the heart of a Loyalist stronghold. The sandbags, the rolls of barbed wire, the high metal cage and the grey barricades were naturally all in position, but the hideous tension within was relieved. Policing the Old Town was still a distasteful business and would always present the same danger, but at least when such forays were over, you could rest and feel at home in a territory where you were lauded and loved, where kerbstones painted red white and blue gave a constant and visible boost to morale.

When we reached the New Barracks today, we were welcomed as if to a sanctuary. The big building was almost deserted, strewn with signs of hasty departure, but despite the emptiness, the place was so charged with excitement that it did not seem abandoned; the air crackled with purpose and energy. We were brought through at once to see Jim, who was sitting with his family in a small room beside the cells, talking to the duty officer. He jumped up when we came in, and greeted us very heartily. The others rose as well, but without his determined exuberance. They looked bemused and dishevelled, and uncertain of what was expected of them. They had not had time to dress, and the children's pyjama collars showed above the necks of their jerseys, Heather's nightdress beneath the thick hem of her coat. They were wearing no socks, and their legs were arrestingly white and skinny above shoes that appeared too large for them, shoes not made for

167

bare feet. We all stared at them, stunned. They looked like refugees, and it took us a moment to master the shock. Then my mother gave a cry of indignation and pity and threw her arms around Heather, and we all began speaking together.

'The children were still in their beds . . .'

'The wickedness! Oh, the wickedness!'

'They're afraid that the house will be damaged.'

'Ach now, if they use the pig-sticks, there'll be no great damage done. They can shoot away the explosive charge.'

'If there is one at all,' said my father. 'Have they found out for certain the thing's not a hoax?'

He looked hopefully at his son, but Jim said soberly, 'I'm afraid so.'

'They wanted to kill Daddy!'

'Well, they haven't, my darling, we're all of us safe.'

'Just let them wait, that's all. Just let them wait till I'm older and they'll see who's doing the killing!'

'That's not Christian talking, Ian.'

Sergeant Gormley appeared at the door, and cleared his throat portentously. 'The Super's here to see you!'

He stood back and Joe Baker strode into the room. His bearing proclaimed to all that he was a busy, important man, who was used to giving orders, but his manner was solicitous. He threw out an arm to Jim and clapped him on the shoulder, and more gravely shook hands with my father – sub-divisional superintendent, maybe, but also a family friend who planned to proceed with delicacy.

'I'm glad to see you,' he said, 'though I'm sorry about the occasion. A chair here for Mr McMurtry! We don't want to keep him standing.' The constable scurried away, and brought one for me too. Jimmy perched on the desk. 'Well, give us the latest,' he said. 'Have you laid your hands on an A.T.O.? Or won't they leave Crossmaglen? Sure a change of view would refresh them.'

Joe grinned. 'There's one on his way, and we're all going

down to the I.C.P. in a minute.' He turned to my father. 'We've an Incident Control Point at the entrance to Folly Lane. You can see both the house and the car from there, and I want you to check some features – on the spot, so to speak.' His eyes swivelled to me. 'Would you come along with us, Alison?' He phrased it as a question, although only one reply could be made to such a suggestion.

'We'll need your statement,' he added, 'with the details about this phone call – but we'll deal with that by and by. We can handle it down at the I.C.P., and that's where we should be at the present.'

'Can I come with you?' cried Ian.

'You'll stay right here by me!' Heather put out her hand, but he shook it off and persisted, made bold by his longing, 'I want to talk to the bomb squad!'

'You're a keen young blade,' said Joe, 'but you're not big enough for this sort of thing yet. You stay here and help Sergeant Gormley.' Ian's face flushed with mortification, and Joe tousled his hair, 'Will this do – I'll send up for you when we get the all clear? And if you come down directly, you can get in a chat with the A.T.O.' He exchanged a wink with Jim. 'So if you'll excuse us, ladies, we must get back to our duty! Sergeant Gormley here will look after you, and the very minute we know that this device is dismantled, we'll be through to you on the blower.'

He waved a clenched fist in a cheerful salute as he moved towards the door, and without further pause for dispute or farewell we found ourselves out in the passage. His authority, total and steely, glinted momentarily through the velvet glove of his friendship, and I knew even Jimmy sensed it as we marched down the narrow corridor. We were doing what we were told, and if one of us had objected we would not have been heard or heeded. But of course no objections were necessary, for we were among our own.

* * *

169

It took time to get down to the I.C.P., though we drove with sirens wailing. Joe explained that the sudden congestion was caused by the one-way traffic flow being interrupted along the Mall.

'We've had to put out a cordon, and the Mall's well within the two hundred yards. The shopping precinct too. Not to mention the telephone exchange, or the bus depot! Jesus, Jimmy! Could you not have lived out in the country?' Though he jested, his face was grim. 'I hate to see this disruption. Playing into their hands for publicity. Now if it had been up at Dunvarden we could have left it to stew, that always disappoints them. But down here! For God's sake, would you look at them!'

He gestured contempt through the window, and we peered out. To our right, we could see that a cordon was in place blocking off the end of a side road, with a small crowd gathering round it. 'By the time we defuse this device, every Taig in the town will be down at the ropes hoping someone will get injured. And it takes half my men to keep them out – they all want a closer view. It would turn your stomach to watch them.'

We ourselves had now passed through the cordon, and drew up in the yard of the bus depot at the end of Folly Lane where the big mobile control point was already in position. We all got out and looked around us. Empty buses stood in rows at the back of the tarmac forecourt where police and army vehicles were bristling with armed activity.

'At least it was early,' said Joe, 'The evacuation was easy enough. No footering round with the public. Just some cleaners and watchmen and skeleton shifts. There'll be some trouble over the phones, for we had to clear out the Exchange pretty fast, and no doubt a fair shortage of buses. It's Shanks's pony for some folks this morning.'

He looked up, and I followed his stare to the flat concrete heights above us. 'The army's got boys up there, securing the rooftops for us, so at least we're decently covered. We could wing every rebel from here to the docks!' he relinquished this thought with a sigh as an officer approached him. 'Here's the CO,' he muttered to Jim, 'nothing he doesn't know, and he's been here a month! I'll introduce you anyway.'

The CO regarded us coldly. Bandit country, and natives were natives. He disliked this big policeman, and it did not matter to him that we were the superintendent's friends. Besides our name had a ring he associated with trouble. Loyalists in a Nationalist town. Protection rackets and murder? Christ! He'd as soon trust mad dogs as these people. It was no job for honest soldiers, propping up this ambiguous role of a peace-keeping force working with the police. He inclined his head stiffly to Joe, and remarked that he hoped everything was in hand, and that the A.T.O. had arrived and wanted to see him.

'Well, that's mutual,' said Joe. 'At this moment there's no one I'd like to see more.'

We followed him through the bus yard. Day had dawned. Someone turned off the floodlamps. Above us, the northern sky spread pale and pure over the fortified roofs. The mountains reared up behind, very clear, very near in the aqueous light. Aloof and ancient and cold, testaments to a far grander timescale, they reduced the scene below to a game of toy guns and tin soldiers. Patriot and friend and foe and invader could pass beneath them, make no mark and receive no blessing, though they fought to the death in their shadow; and I felt myself pierced to the bone by that exquisite barb I could never deflect. Sure you're soft, Ginger! What's to be made outa them bare ould hills? Even sheep die up there . . .

I dropped my gaze and shuddered. Unexpectedly, Jim linked a thick arm though mine. 'It'll not take long now,' he said. 'Here's your man and his paraphernalia!' He nodded towards Folly Lane and the Land Rover parked between two armoured cars. It was drawing a camouflaged trailer, and a cluster of uniformed men stood around as its contents were

171

brought down the ramp. A young soldier in combat dress came across to us and saluted.

'Reporting for duty,' he said, 'Ammunitions Technical Officer, sir!'

The CO actually smiled, and for the first time looked quite human. 'Glad to see you, Sergeant Ridley. I don't want to hold up operations, but before you get ready to go, the police think the owners should take a quick look.'

He indicated us briefly, and his tone and the look in his eyes ridiculed our interference. But here he found no collusion: Sergeant Ridley was clearly not new to the job, and on excellent terms with Joe, and the two slapped shoulders genially. Formal introductions were made, jokes exchanged, field glasses issued. We all went forward together, and stared down Folly Lane at my brother's back gate and the yard beyond. We had a clear view of the Rover, parked alongside the house up against the back door.

'Well, what did I tell you?' said Jim. 'She's practically in the kitchen! If she goes up a lot will go with her.'

'Well, she shouldn't go up,' said the A.T.O. 'With luck we'll defuse the explosive. There's a pretty good chance with a pig-stick. We'll send the wheelbarrow in, and get as close as we can to her.'

Joe Baker turned to Jim. 'But I wanted you to see her first, and appreciate the problem. Things can go wrong very easily, and she's right by the house as you see. That is where you put her yourself, by the way?'

Jimmy nodded at him glumly. 'It was coming down like the clappers. Quite a price to pay for dry skin!' He turned awkwardly to my father. 'I'm sorry about the car, Pop. If you hadn't lent her to me, this would never have happened to her.'

'I don't know about that, son. Maybe somebody thought that the Rover was the right place to put a car bomb. She's

172

like part of the firm now, we've had her so long. Or like part of the family.'

'Well, all the more reason to save her.' Joe handed the field glasses over to Jim. 'You should be able to see a box underneath the chassis? Right? That's not part of your fixtures and fittings? A special place for your sandwiches?'

Jimmy, down on his hands and knees, shook his head in reply. 'The bastards! I'd crucify the lot of them.' He stood up again, ugly with anger. 'What I would like to see is a few of them put in that car and despatched for a taste of their own medicine. I'd consider my house was a small price to pay.'

Nobody answered him; though we all groped for words, none seemed fitting. Even Joe's black humour failed, and my father stifled his protests. The efforts we had made to behave with cheerful decorum were not suitable any longer. We withdrew from each other by common consent. The A.T.O. went away to check out his equipment, and put on his ceramic armour. Joe set out on a tour of his cordons. I suggested tentatively that my father might find it more restful sitting down inside the control point, but as I expected, he turned down this move. We huddled uncomfortably on the tailboard of a lorry, too divided by separate tensions to provide further help for each other.

Joe came back eventually, and declared that the action was starting, we had grandstand seats here and no question . . . The morning, already unreal, now took on the quality of a science-fiction film. The familiar became unstable. The known view through Jim's gate, his square house, the old car, Ian's bicycle under the window, the corner of Heather's rosebed – these solid reliable things had become cardboard backdrops for what was afoot. We were feverish, dreaming, deluded. We were watching a horror movie. We saw the A.T.O., now transformed from a man to a monstrous lump of space-walker's padded clothing, waddle out, side by side

173

with a robot on tracks, and stand there in Folly Lane like a creature from some other planet. As he turned his faceless head, the sun flashed brightly off his visor. The machine in front of him wriggled, and began to advance at a spirited lurch.

'By jeepers, there she goes! Do you see the wee camera mounted up front?' Joe Baker nudged Jim eagerly, like a child showing off a mechanical toy. 'It's remote controlled TV – so your man can position the shotgun dead on. Great jobs, these wheelbarrow geezers!' But for once, Jim did not share his ardour. He watched impassively as the thing jolted past the gateposts. A long cable unwound behind it, its extendable boom waved around like a wand, but its ludicrous gait belied a precision and power that we knew to be there; and despite his clumsy clothing, the A.T.O. guided it deftly.

'A mercury-tilt,' said Joe, looking up from his walkie-talkie, 'but he doesn't like the look of it. Awkward place and awkward angle.'

The boom was now under the Rover. Messages passed to and fro. Sergeant Ridley conferred with his closed circuit set. The sharpness had left the sky, and the mountains lost colour: rain wasn't far off.

'Well, he's going to give it a try.'

'He hasn't much alternative.'

'Sure it's only an old car, Jimmy, and a bit of bricks and mortar.'

'And I should have been inside – or Alison, as it so happens. And the children in the kitchen! I'll have them for this, if it costs me my life!'

'Dear God!' my father cried. 'Is there no end to this perversion?'

He threw out his hand to Jim in a gesture of desperate entreaty, but his next words were carried away by a massive detonation that echoed from building to building, and shook

174

the ground beneath us. An orange ball of flame engulfed the place where the Rover had stood. Its doors burst upwards and outwards. Splintered glass showered aloft like a fountain. Lumps of metal soared into the sky, as though harmless and weightless as snowflakes.

Even standing by Patsy's bed, the sheer physical experience of destruction had not come to me. I had known it then with my head, with my mind and my emotions: now I felt it in my flesh, in my limbs and my stomach and thundering heart. I seemed blasted bodily. I was part of the debris that whirled through the air. Yet beneath me, time was suspended. I could see myself by the lorry; Jim, a sentence half begun, his mouth open to complete it; Joe, his ear to his radio transmitter, Sergeant Ridley's hand pressed to the trigger; and unforgettably – etched dark against the exploding car like some stern old testament prophet, the figure of my father with his hand outstretched to his son.

'Right, Alison,' said Joe Baker, 'so you heard the telephone ringing. Did you take the time exactly?'

'It was six o'clock,' I said. 'I was asleep and it woke me.'

The man from the CID wrote studiously in his note book. The young woman constable smiled at me. It was all as informal as possible. We were seated comfortably in a small office requisitioned from the Ulster bus headquarters. Through the window just beside me I could see the I.C.P., where my father and Jimmy were waiting their turn to come over and make their statements. Jim had not cared for this arrangement. He had said rather testily it was like the inquisition. Can't you just write down what happened, it's the same whoever tells it? Joe had answered pleasantly that he felt more might come from three separate chats; all discrepancies were revealing; and you'd never believe, till you heard it yourself, how folks' statements could vary and change. Anyway, he'd see Alison now, ladies first . . . But looking across the desk, I could not believe gallantry guided his choice.

'Now, in your own words,' he said, 'could you tell me exactly what happened.'

I wondered could I get away with some sort of general statement? I said quickly, 'It was a warning. I was told that a bomb had been put in the car.'

'In the car?'

'Well, in the Rover. And I telephoned Jim, as the Rover was there. I rang up the barracks as well. My poor father came down; he had heard the phone too.' What else had my father heard, and how much would he tell when questioned? 'That's the gist of it,' I said, and was pleased that my voice sounded shaky and faint. Ladies first. A poor widow woman. He might let me go now, no decisions, no lies.

'Bring some water for Mrs Lacey.' He examined his nails while I took a few sips. Then he said, 'Look, it's tough on you, Alison, you've been through a bad experience; but you've got to try again. There's a lot in this warning that doesn't add up. Now – you picked up the phone and you said?'

'I said, this is Dunvarden.'

'Go on.'

Jeez, I thought I'd missed ye! Are you still for Antrim this morning? And if I'd denied it, what then? Would my brother have gone to a hideous death? Who was Colm, that I should protect him? A murderer and a terrorist.

I tried a half-truth again. 'A man said, "Don't go anywhere near the big car." Then he said, "Don't touch the Rover!"'

Joe said sharply, 'This voice! Please describe it.'

I could hear Colm's voice all too well, gruff with urgency, husky with terror, the thick speech of a man who is juggling with hope, fear and shame. 'Alison? Are ye there? Keep away from the Rover, I'm telling you straight.' A man betraying his

176

friends, his ideals, his love for his country, all because he has found in the end that he cannot kill someone he knew as a child.

I said, 'He sounded . . . frightened.'

Joe repeated, reflectively, 'frightened?'

Though he spoke quite amiably, I saw instantly that the word was wrong. I had not been aware till then of the depth of my pity for Colm, and I had displayed it rashly. Pity clearly was inappropriate. Well, it could not be unsaid; after all, I was meant to be speaking the truth.

I attempted some redress. 'It was an Irish accent.'

'From the South, you mean?'

'No, it was Northern, I think.' Badly put – this had not pleased Joe, though the slip was accidental.

'Can you be more precise? Was it local?'

I was suddenly panic-stricken. If I said yes, the path was plain to admitting the voice was familiar, and yet if I answered no, I was committed to lying. I found it hard to think clearly; I could still feel explosion along every nerve. Only one certainty remained as I struggled through this new turmoil: that the bomb had been meant for my brother, and it might have destroyed his whole family. I thought of them now, torn apart as grotesquely as my father's car.

I must not misdirect this policeman.

'Yes,' I said, 'I think it was local.'

A change came over Joe, and I knew that he too sensed a turning-point. He leaned forward on his desk, with the balls of his fingers together. 'What I don't understand,' he said, 'is why they phoned Dunvarden. The Rover was down at Jimmy's, and the warning was otherwise accurate – doubtless one of their own boyos, out looking to earn a few brownie points before he gets arrested. Have you any ideas on the matter at all? Take your time.'

I had never considered this. Now I wondered. Had Colm known that the Rover was not at Dunvarden? It was I, not

177

he, who had said so. Had he simply been told that the big car was fixed?

I said slowly, 'Well, I suppose the informer might not have been in on the job? If he'd found out – or if he'd been told that the Rover had been booby-trapped, he'd assume it was up at Dunvarden.'

'I don't find that very convincing.'

I said, 'Mistakes happen, Joe. Perhaps they meant to ring Jimmy. We're side by side in the phone book.'

'No other explanations?' and when I shook my head, he went on quietly, 'I've a notion. It's no more than a hunch at the minute, but I'd like to discuss it with you.'

He was looking closely at me, and I saw he was taking my measure; he was wondering just how defenceless I was. He was assessing me for delayed shock and nervous exhaustion, and I knew with a cold certainty that he wanted me very defenceless indeed. He needed a hold over me that was hard to achieve, since I was who I was. Now, of course if I had been Colm, there'd have been other ways of approaching the job . . . Abruptly, vividly, I saw Joe Baker standing beside the canal, the soft voice, the hard eyes, the strong body, and the small writhing boy with his arm twisted back.

I tried to look attentive. Joe was speaking. 'I see it this way – if that call hadn't come, you'd have been for the chop; and I don't think that was intended. But then nobody knew you were taking the car. Or did they?'

I said nothing.

'Or did somebody know of it, Alison? I would like you, if you please, to think very carefully on that point. Did you mention to anyody you'd be driving the Rover this morning?'

'Well, of course my family . . .'

'I mean, apart from your family.'

Thon's a heavy auld bus to be driving . . . I'm for Antrim in the morning, scrake of dawn, so I'd better get used to it . . .

Despite everything you say, there are fair laws and decent policemen . . . If they could pin it on me, they'd be only too delighted. They've got some old scores to settle . . . I'd crucify the lot of them . . . The bastards! . . . My country is Ireland . . .

But the mould had been cracked. I was here, still alive.

'I can't remember,' I said.

'Think again. Things come back.' Threat lurked somewhere, far off. 'It's a matter of great importance. If we're going to nail these bastards, then we need a lead right away. If we could lift your caller, we'd be able to squeeze something out of him,' I winced, and I saw Joe's mouth tighten. He changed direction again. 'Let's go back to the bomb warning. You say the voice was local. Well, think hard. Did you recognise it?'

The seconds ticked, clicked away. I remembered the noise on the telephone line. Colm had been using a phone box. I could see, I could smell him standing there, with his coins and his guilt and his fright; the damp cigarette stubs, the scrawled words on the walls, the odour of stale beer and urine, and of his own sweating terror. I could feel the watchful night, the alert hostile dark the informer knows, clawing round the misted windows. I felt once and for all the unbearable weight of the price he had paid for my life.

I looked into Joe's face, and our eyes met and held. He had not forgotten the schoolbag, nor the fact that I had married a Catholic. And his guts told him straight and plain that I was hiding something. Nonetheless, I was Jimmy's sister, and why, surely-to-God, after what had been done? All this his expression contained, and still it remained hopeful.

I dearly wished I could please him. I did not court his uncomprehending contempt. His clan was by blood my clan, as it was my mother's and Jimmy's; as a child I had known its protection, its strong tribal support in a treacherous world. Now my birthright was offered again and I could not

179

accept its comfort, its convictions or its fellowship. I abjured them with infinite sadness.

I said, 'I'm sorry Joe. I have absolutely no idea who it was, or why they phoned me. I wish I could do more to help you.'

I turned my head away. I should have looked at him squarely, but I knew myself faithless, a traitor. I did not want to see what he thought of me as I sat before him and lied.

When my father came out from his meeting with Joe, we were offered a lift to the barracks. 'You'll want to get back to the womenfolk. We'll bring up Mr Jim when he's done talking to the Super.' But my father said stoutly, no, he wanted to see the damage first, and how could we reassure Heather without knowing the state of the back of her house?

We walked down Folly Lane in unaccustomed silence. No one made any move to stop us. They had put out the fire and completed the search. Soldiers watched indifferently as we came through the gate – one more thankless task done, and this time no casualties, not even among the locals – but several policemen approached us,

'Shockin' business, sir. I'm sorry.'

'Ach Wesley! Praises be there's none of his family injured!'

'Sure, they say troubles never come singly! The auld house has stood up till it powerfully well.'

We looked up at the glassless windows, the charred eaves, the earth-square that was once the back porch.

'Nothin' wrong there that can't be mended! The big car's had her chips though, no doubt about that.'

'Fuckin' bastards!'

'Ladies present!'

'I beg your pardon, Missus.'

They withdrew to a tactful distance as we stared at the wreck of the Rover. The doors had been blown off their hinges, the roof buckled, the bonnet thrown open; the crumpled steering-wheel lay on what remained of the engine. There was no sign of any upholstery, and the tyres had vanished completely. The chassis was blackened by flame from the petrol tank, and the air was rank.

We stood quietly, as if at a graveside. Then my father smiled shakily, 'I don't think Billy's garage will make much of that.'

He went forward, reverently, and laid his hand on his tortured car. 'She felt like a friend,' he said, 'but your mother would say that was fanciful, and she's right. Well, it's no good lamenting. You're alive, and that's all that matters.'

He picked up a lump of glass, now thick and smooth-edged from the heat of the blaze, and vaguely turned it over. We did not look at each other. The police had opened the Mall, and the noise was isolating; it proclaimed this an ordinary morning, with a bit of a rumpus around Killycreel – dirty Brits, or bloody Taigs, depending how you looked at it. I longed to escape this insanity, to take my father with me; yet beside this grim hulk in Jim's yard, the longing had no reality. The memory of Ben, of my home and my child and the life that I loved, seemed impossibly, frighteningly distant.

'You were in a long time with Joe Baker?' He spoke with his back half turned. 'He was done with me pretty quickly.'

I opened my mouth to reply, and then shut it again. I had thought of this, yes – of the huge risk that I was taking in assuming my father was quite unaware that I knew who had been on that phone; but my moral dilemma had pushed it aside. Now its full implications came home with a horrifying impact.

I said hoarsely, 'He wanted to know if I'd any idea who the warning was from. I told him I couldn't help him.' I could hear the embarrassing break in my voice.

My father glanced up from the rubble. 'That's my girl,' he said with pride, and his face showed no sign of surprise or dismay; he looked suddenly stronger, younger. He turned briskly away from the Rover, and took my hand. 'Don't you cry – you'll have the two of us at it. It's a very lonely road, but we don't need to go down it weeping. Come on, and I'll take you home.'

He hesitated a moment, and then he added sombrely, 'I'll do Colm no harm, you can rest sure of that. God protect him from his own.'

I met Charlie Glencreagh in the entrance hall on the day of the Old Masters auction. He was staying in Ireland for Easter, and had caught the first flight from Belfast. He came straight to the sale from the airport.

'You shouldn't have bothered, Charlie.'

'Oh, no bother! I always intended to come. In fact, the silly thing was I'd arranged to be here yesterday, for the view. Quite forgotten the Ravenscroft wedding. Now it's going to be rather a rush, I'm afraid.'

'Oh, there's heaps of time, don't worry. It doesn't start till eleven.' I gave his airline bag to the porter behind the reception desk. 'You've got a catalogue?'

He nodded, patting his briefcase. 'In here somewhere, if I can find it. Thought the photos came out rather well in the end, didn't you? Surprisingly striking. Though of course, nothing does them justice.' He glanced at me hopefully, 'I suppose none of them is still hanging?'

'No,' I said, 'I'm awfully sorry. They'll be round at the back, all stacked up for the sale.' His face fell: he wanted his paintings, and to see them while he could still call them his own. I went on, 'I could take you through, but there's really no point now they're not on the wall.'

'No. Of course not. It doesn't matter.' He was gracious in his disappointment.

I said hastily, 'By the way, things look as though they're improving. There's been quite a lot of interest.'

'Oh, there has?' As I hoped, he brightened. The market had grown depressed and been very unstable since Christmas. He was certainly well aware it was not a good time to be selling, but he needed to go ahead much more urgently than he was pleased to admit. He had four pictures in this sale, and we both knew he would be lucky if they managed to reach their reserve price.

'Well, in that case I'm glad I'm not missing the fun.' His voice was crisp again, detached and almost perfunctory, and he changed the subject smoothly, 'I must say, it's been lovely in Ireland. Did you manage to get away for a bit of a break over Easter?'

'Yes. We spent it in France,' I said. 'We stayed with some friends in Normandy.'

'Oh?' He sounded vaguely offended. 'Well, you certainly missed the good weather at home, blue skies day after day. Can't remember such a perfect Spring.'

'So I hear. I was over earlier.'

I had been back twice since Christmas. The black ice of January's frost, and the February floods that had closed the coast road had been the least of my worries. My mother looked smaller and thinner; my father, though outwardly calm, was suffering from headaches. There had been no arrest for the car-bomb attack. Trouble smouldered down at the yards where the men were complaining about the restraints of the tightened security measures. Jim and Heather had moved to the bungalow, and had fitted burglar alarms in their new home and at Dunvarden – 'Just a cod,' confided my father, 'but don't tell your mother I said so. See this fancy little bell? You're supposed to say to the gunman, "Just you wait a minute, sonny, while I run for my panic button." ' He had laughed, fingering his head where the scar still showed a dull purple. 'Such tomfoolery! Still, if it pleases them . . .' All the merriment died from his voice and his eyes and he added wearily, 'Maybe play-acting's better than nothing at all.' Afterwards it occurred to me that this play-acting extended to much more than the panic button. There was little left that was natural in his strained relations with Jim, or the cheerful façade that he showed to his wife.

I returned guiltily to Charlie.

'As a matter of fact,' he was saying, 'it's been so particularly fine that we've taken the plunge and begun on the roof. I've got hold of a marvellous builder.' I attempted a smile of solicitude, but he turned my concern away with a nonchalant shrug of the shoulders, 'Well, one can't wait around for ever. Let's just hope today proves exciting.'

'I'm sure it will,' I said, picking up my lead politely, and hoping I sounded convincing. I glanced down at my watch, 'Still got half an hour left. There's an interesting preview upstairs that might keep you amused while you're waiting.'

We began to elbow our way up the wide marble steps to the first-floor rooms. The stairwell was rich with colour, hung with prayer mats and embroideries reserved for a future sale. Tapestries were draped over the bannisters, Persian wall-hangings dangled beneath them, quilts and carpets were piled up at random on the circular gallery rail underneath the big crystal chandelier. The lots for tomorrow's sale of French and Italian furniture dominated the rest of the landing, an ornate and elaborate sideshow. We were running two auctions today, Old Masters and musical instruments, and the anteroom was crowded. A few people were starting to trickle away to the salerooms on either side, but most were still meeting and greeting here, local buyers, Americans, Frenchmen, Japanese and Arabs and Germans.

I glanced backwards at Charlie Glencreagh, noting he was already engrossed in the scene. I felt warmed by his obvious pleasure. I liked him better in London. The ill-fitting Irishness that had seemed so absurd at Drumgarvey, was less irksome and obtrusive in this cosmopolitan gathering. The Old Masters' clientele absorbed him without effort; a number of them were dressed, just as he was, in suits of conventional cut, and these melted in with the rest, with the elegant and the exotic in their smart couturier labels, and the consciously arty in casual clothes that veered from velvet and lace to aggressively faded denims. Among these butterflies, the musical instrument buyers in their unpretentious garments looked collected and pedestrian, yet the fever in the air had imprinted all their faces with the tension of the exam room, with the same fear of failure of judgment or nerve. The fortune was still to be made; the competitors braced at the starting gate. None of those attending the sales had the time or inclination to take in the objects around them, but a few of tomorrow's customers moved about in a businesslike way, minutely inspecting the furniture.

As I watched Charlie squeeze between them, I wondered how soon I could leave him? I would find him a seat at the sale, and slip off when the bidding got into its swing. There was much to be done in my office, and I wanted to get back to it. I was keen to get away as soon as I could this evening. When I came home yesterday, Robin told me my father had telephoned from the yards, but had left no message, and I hoped that tonight he might ring me again. Every now and then, these days, he would phone me like this from his office, and although it was never admitted that such calls were deliberately private, they were in a different key from the studiously commonplace family chats we endured when he spoke from Dunvarden, and their intimacy was precious. It always worried me if I failed to be there when he phoned from the yards . . .

'Well, good Lord!' I heard Charlie say, and I saw he was gazing sardonically at a mighty Flemish cabinet, squat and heavy with prosperity, inlaid with black and red, much gilded

185

and silver mounted. It had a dowager's presence. Charlie read aloud from the notice, 'Mid-eighteenth century. Important boulle cabinet-on-stand'. He raised one eyebrow at me. 'I suppose that's one way of putting it!'

I smiled vaguely. 'Well, look around you – you'll find most things here are "important"! It's a very useful adjective. If you're stuck for words in the trade it can cover a multitude of sins.' Yes, a poorly proportioned cupboard. I stared at it, my thoughts still in Killycreel. 'I'm afraid my father would say he had never beheld such an ignorant press.'

I paused, wishing the words unspoken. I had not meant to mention my father. Some sort of routine exchange about matters in Northern Ireland was no doubt inevitable, but I'd hoped to delay it as long as I could. Now through absent-mindedness, I had unmistakably prompted one.

Quick to take his cue, Charlie said, 'And how about your family? Rotten time they all had before Christmas. It must be a terrible worry for you?' As he spoke, he bent forward and gazed at two ebony ormolu *bibliothèques*. 'Louis Quinze – they're rather lovely.'

'Yes,' I said, hoping this answered both remarks.

'Killycreel's a tricky place.' He stopped short, but I made no comment. Ludicrously, I felt affronted. Of course Killycreel was a nightmare, but to hear it criticised by outsiders with English accents jarred.

Charlie disregarded my silence, and the disapproval it carried. He repeated, 'A tricky place. And a tricky situation.' The bookcases seemed very absorbing, and he opened the doors and examined the shelves, adding with averted face, 'Have they ever thought of moving?'

'You're not talking about my parents?' I let scorn for this folly conceal my real shock.

'Well, yes. Yes, I was.' Charlie said. 'Can't be pleasant for them down that way any more.'

'But it isn't "down that way"! Not to them. It's their home.' Pride fought fear, and pride won. Must I listen to such nonsense, to such preposterous rubbish? 'They'd as soon go to Timbuktu as move away from the district.'

'Even so, maybe you should suggest it.' He looked up from the polished ebony. The deadly seriousness of what he was trying to tell me broke through his airy manner and flared undisguised between us. 'It's not a healthy place. Not these days. And not for your parents.'

I said coldly, 'You don't know my parents. You don't understand their position. What on earth do you think they'd do – cut adrift from their home and their work and their friends?' I stared sullenly at my tormentor. I did not want to start a catalogue of how my family had invested in harbour and port and canal; of how tenaciously they had built up the town they had founded, and administered its fortunes. One had only to look at them to know they were rooted in the clay far too deeply for any transplanting. 'They're as much part of Killycreel as the lough itself.'

Charlie stood his ground. 'That may be true,' he said, 'but they'd be a darned sight safer if they left! All these feuds and vendettas! It's reprisal and counter-reprisal down there. There's hardly a week goes by that you don't hear of some new atrocity. Even in this morning's paper –'

I broke in with bad manners I could not restrain. 'I'm aware of all that, thank you! I don't need anyone to remind me!'

Could he not see it made no difference? My father preparing for Patsy's wake, 'My duty's perfectly plain, and I'm nobody's puppet, Alison'. My mother turning to wave to the staff gathered round the Infirmary steps, 'There's no better place to be living. Where else would you find such loyalty?' Jimmy thumping the hospital bed. 'You're an Ulsterman like I am!' No.

I said, 'They'll stay there if it kills them.' My voice trembled on the catch-phrase. It was horrible to say such a thing when the words could be accurate.

I stared down at the Turkish carpet. I tried to fix my attention on the legs passing to and fro, on the forest of pinstripes and stockings and boots, on the glinting edge of a sari, but calm refused to come to me. This beautiful opulent room where I always had found a respite from my worries about Dunvarden was no longer a refuge from panic and dread. The air had become imbued with a stifling claustrophobia, and I deeply resented my client as the carrier of this pestilence. I knew I had been rude, and that all my reactions were wholly unjust in the face of well-meaning counsel, but this did not help the matter. There was nothing to be done but effect a quick change of subject.

'It's a hopeless case,' I said, striving clumsily for a lighter tone, 'You'd have more chance of shifting the mountains. We'd far better look at the furniture.'

I stood back to let two Japanese pass between us to go to the instrument sale, and was very thankful to see my companion obediently turn away to an exquisite bowfronted bureau.

'I should think this must be Italian?'

I nodded gratefully, 'And this time genuinely "important".' We admired the olivewood's patina, the subtle changes of colour in the fruitwood marquetry, and the happy conjunction of straight line and bow. Reticence and courtesy were established again between us, and I vowed they would not be disrupted. This was no time for family problems. I would shut out Killycreel and the quicksand it represented. By the time we went into the saleroom, my professional bearing was almost restored.

We settled strategically on the aisle at the back, giving Charlie a seat that was well placed for watching the bidding, and myself an easy exit. I looked round appraisingly, and was satisfied by the attendance; chairs were full, buyers fingered their dockets, conversation was earnest and faces alert. This sale could never be a sensational occasion in the terms of a leading auction house, but the lots were of solid quality, and the air of expectancy in the crowded room was indicative of a market prepared for action; Charlie's pictures might fare rather well after all. Now that I was more at ease, and he correspondingly nervous, I felt almost protective towards him, and hoped very much they would do so. In this avid company he seemed curiously guileless, less the seasoned city banker than the indigent aristocrat confronting a den of thieves, and I feared that his plight was in some part my fault.

I said reassuringly, 'We've got an excellent turnout.'

'Do you think so? I hope they mean business. We've got one pretty near the beginning.' His briefcase was on his knee, and he opened it as he was speaking. 'Lot eleven, if I'm not mistaken. Where the devil is my catalogue?'

'Here, have mine!'

'Oh, no . . . honestly! Look, I've found it.' He brought out the magazine and the Belfast morning paper, 'And what's more, here's the *Telegraph*, fresh from the press! Latest news from the home country! First edition and free on the morning flight! I thought you might like to see it.' As I took it his flippancy faded, and he added uncomfortably, 'More unpleasantness round Killycreel, I'm afraid. Though thank God, not to do with your people.'

He broke off, for a hush had fallen. The auctioneer of the day had come in and mounted the rostrum. A local daily paper was no longer a thing of immediate concern. Two porters had made their way to the stand at the front, and all eyes were turned to the painting they placed upon it. The international moneyboard flickered into life. Lot one. Pounds, dollars, francs, yen and deutschmarks. Beneath it the staff assembled, pencils poised and phones at the ready.

The picture that opened the sale was an eighteenth-century landscape in a neo-classical style, with figures illustrating a literary fable. Two lovers under a tree (Angelica and Medoro, so I understood from my cataglogue) neither seemed to have captured the painter's heart, nor entirely set it free to concentrate on the background; as they languished insipidly in their unconvincing setting and the bidding gathered momentum, Charlie gave me a barely perceptible wink. If this painting sold handsomely when we both found it weak and derivative, it would surely set a precedent? The stark future was suddenly glinting with gold. He leaned forward eagerly as the twenty thousand mark was reached, and the prices began to rise faster.

'Twenty-two I am bid.

'Twenty-five at the back.

'Twenty-eight. Are there any advances? Twenty-eight thousand pounds, and it's here on the left.'

From the rostrum, gimlet eyes flickered round us in instant assessment. The desire to win the prize is increased by the fear that a moment's delay may rob you of it for ever, and this tempo is set from the very first lot. A good auctioneer never wastes time, and Ned Seymour was known for his accurate pace and command of mood. Charlie might frown as the gavel tapped the rostrum, but its reprimand was deliberate, and a new urgent appetite quickened the room. By the time lot eleven came round, Ned had whetted it into a hunger. He allowed his razor smile to skate briefly over his captives. 'I may say this exceptional painting has aroused a lot of interest.'

We all knew these words implied that commissioned bids on the picture were already satisfactory, and that it was worth all we could offer and more. The room braced itself for

190

a fight, for it saw for itself that this claim was true – Charlie's van der Neer was delightful, a limpid translucent landscape with the characteristic glow of a masterly oil on oak panel. Its small scale and richness of texture made its modest structure a virtue. The marshland, the tranquil sky, the cows grouped under the farmstead, and the windmill in the background formed a simple composition, but the painting drew the eye as though it were a jewel.

Charlie shifted restlessly, and I knew he was torn between sorrow and greed. His main hopes of gain lay with this picture, but he felt its loss all the more keenly for that. As I watched him crane awkwardly in his efforts to catch a last glimpse of it, I felt an embarrassed pity both for him and for his painting; in the anonymity of an auction room, both seemed forsaken – and yet, disloyally, I felt burdened by their presence. Charlie's words of advice echoed bleakly. On its stand in front of the auctioneer, the moonlit estuary that should have conveyed such serenity simply threw me back into the turmoil I had known as I packed and crated it in the stately gallery at Drumgarvey House. Though I struggled to cling to the reassuring present, it no longer held all my attention. The unwelcome memory of a dislocated afternoon at the start of a lonely journey drifted in and out of my consciousness; I could smell the damp air from the sea, feel the polished floor of the ballroom where I knelt among the shavings, taste the sour aftermath of ordeal in my mouth. I admonished myself angrily for such weakness and indiscipline. I must concentrate on the bidding.

'Twenty-five thousand pounds on the aisle to my right.

'Twenty-eight on the telephone.

'Thirty thousand with me.'

A scant nod from his staff had revealed the first commission, and the room was aware it would not be the last. If Ned claimed that 'interest' was shown, then you did not expect a bargain, you were ready for drastic action. A warning was a warning ... 'A tricky place, Killycreel. Have they ever thought of moving?' We'd had warnings enough in all conscience ...

'Thirty-two.

'Thirty-five.

'Thirty-eight by the door.'

The room hummed, and I strove desperately to remain within its confines. I did not look back at the painting, or at Charlie Glencreagh beside me, by now more real to me in the library at Drumgarvey than he was on his seat in the saleroom. Instead, I glanced down at my hands on my lap. They seemed oddly divorced from me, loosely clasped on the *Belfast Telegraph*. I had forgotten the paper, and the sight of it lying there gripped me. It was folded meticulously, and I stared mesmerised at the quartered page. It was partly printed in colour, in the gaudy shades of the fairground. A small rectangle of red at the top of the sheet showed a terrorist in a balaclava helmet, with the word MURDER written above him. 'You can help to stop it,' it said, 'use the confidential telephone.' Beneath the Freephone number was a column outlined in forget-me-not blue. A photograph of the Glens bore a caption in pink, 'Wishing you were here ... SEE INSIDE! Follow Hugh McIlwaine as he takes a trip round Cushendun.' I smiled, thinking of my mother, who would not have found humour or paradox here. I allowed my eyes to stray to the black and white of the morning's news. In the centre of the page, which for me was the bottom corner, half a headline in bold print was visible: IRA CLAIMS DISCIPLINARY KILLING. No rare event. Yet today the blood drummed in my ears as I looked at the words. I heard Ned Seymour say 'Fifty thousand with me', but I felt no response to the mounting air of excitement. It was altogether removed from me. I was quite alone, shut away, petrified by a strange icy stillness.

'I don't think Grandad felt like talking.'

'Keep away from the Rover, I'm telling you straight!'

'More trouble down your way, though thank God, not to do with your people.'

IRA CLAIMS DISCIPLINARY KILLING

But there might be no connection. It could be anywhere. Anyone. Any time. Any murder. When I turned the paper over, I would find that my fears were unfounded. Why did I sit and stare at this not unusual sentence as though I confronted a spectre? There were plenty of other informers ...

Although I was well aware that my manners would seem deplorable, and I might interrupt the bidding, I was able to wait no longer. I twisted round in my chair and unfolded the page at arm's length by my side. It was difficult to see, with the paper held low in the shadow like this, and so it was furtively and with straining eyes that I picked out the words that told me of Colm's killing. New Victim of Punishment Shooting. Dead Man from Killycreel. Here the print, growing smaller, became indistinct, but I hardly need its guidance. It was all familiar territory; the bound hands, the sack over the head, the shots from behind. I had no need to read that the body was that of a Catholic, a married man with two children, or to learn that his family were no strangers to terrorist violence. Through the wavering words I could see a myriad of Colms. They changed fast and chaotically, now complete and now mutilated. Rain turned to blood on the heather. The small ragged boy damming the river spun round and revealed to me a maimed face, stripped bare of its features. He lurched forward, and instantly he became a grown man in acute distress, with his hands manacled behind him, and a terrible message to proffer. Before he could speak to me, he was down on his knees by a smouldering car in the rubble of Nanny's cottage, a limp mass with two bullet holes drilled through its back. As the mountains and gunmetal sea rolled over me and engulfed me, I knew that I had killed him. I sat very still as the sickness passed.

'And it's still at seventy! To the gentleman here, with the yellow bow tie.'

At what moment had I condemned him? When I stood with my father at Patsy's wake? When I faced him deliberately with a half-forgotten childhood? But it had not been forgotten; I had seen proof of that in the Convent Square. Had I killed him, then, long ago, when I championed him with a schoolbag against boys of my own persuasion? When I swore I would never sing Orangemen's songs? And if I had betrayed him to Joe at the end of it all, would he still be alive, shielded by police protection? Had my last act of loyalty robbed him of hope?

Horror darkened my mind. Despair overwhelmed my convictions. Perhaps Jimmy's way was better? The unequivocal values. The bigotry nursed and fed to produce a poison specific to one clearly definable species. The sweet conscience of the fanatic. Both Patsy and Colm were dead because simple rules had been flouted – simple rules that ensured survival. Without them and their protection, the hate and the terror had spread to invade family and brotherhood.

'And it's back on my left, as you see! Are there any more offers at seventy-five?'

By what authority, by what right had we disregarded them? Colm's death was upon my head, just as Pat's was upon my father's . . .

Somewhere far off the gavel fell with a small hollow click of authority, and I heard it in my bedlam. Through the tumult and the confusion, it rang crisp and final and cold, a rebuke for abject disorder. 'If you carry on down this road, you must do so with your eyes open.' Colm's eyes had never

194

been closed, not to malice, not to danger. The wary child I had known had grown into an adult well versed in the ways of his country and his people. There was no blindness here, no mistake, no mishap. Not an unexpected death, but the logical outcome of sacrifice . . .

'My God, that was tremendous!' Charlie's fists were clenched tight as he pummelled his thighs, and I focused on him with an effort. I must congratulate him. There were words that should be said to acknowledge a client's good fortune. But for once I could not find them. I stared at him vacantly, stupidly. I was paralysed, possessed by the thought of a sodden body in a ditch beside the border, the discredited corpse of a renegade. Such a death had never led to the making of a hero. There would be no honours for Colm, no national flag on his coffin, no stirring service led by an outraged Bishop O'Brádaigh. If his wife and mother bewailed him, they would do so in shame and in secret. The rest of his terrified clan would be quick to repudiate him. 'Sure, you niver knew what he was thinkin'. It's a mercy the father's been gathered.' Greater love indeed hath no man than to lay down his life for the enemy that has been appointed for him. No greater contempt and rejection can he suffer than the brand of deserter to which he submits himself.

'Lot twelve! As you can see, these paintings form a triptych . . .'

'Aye, but we was like brother and sister.'

'I say, is there something the matter?'

Angrily, I shake my head. I will not cry for Colm. I will not pity my father. That would be an unseemly indulgence. Resolution and bravery are a matter for rejoicing, not for tears, and I will not belittle them with gratuitous grief and compassion. But I mourn for a sad country that can find no place for forbearance among its many virtues. I mourn for a

195

good that is twisted. I am wakened from my sleep by a figure against a blazing sky – 'Is there no end to this perversion?' – and I do not hear an answer. And it is then I weep.